M000236223

SLIP SOUL

A NOVEL

TAYLOR GARCIA

Relax. Read. Repeat.

SLIP SOUL
By Taylor García
Published by TouchPoint Press
Brookland, AR 72417
www.touchpointpress.com

Copyright © 2021 Taylor Garcia
All rights reserved.

ISBN-13: 978-1-952816-68-0

This is a work of fiction. Names, places, characters, and events are fictitious.
Any similarities to actual events and persons, living or dead, are purely
coincidental. Any trademarks, service marks, product names, or named
features are assumed to be the property of their respective owners and are
used only for reference. If any of these terms are used, no endorsement is
implied. Except for review purposes, the reproduction of this book, in whole
or part, electronically or mechanically, constitutes a copyright violation.
Address permissions and review inquiries to media@touchpointpress.com.

Editor: Analieze Cervantes
Cover Design: David Ter-Avanesyan, Ter33Design
Cover Images: Open doorway by Kevin Carden (Adobe Stock); Street of
Oaxaca city at sunrise with its colonial style architecture, Oaxaca state,
Mexico by SL-Photography (Shutterstock); The image of two people in love
at sunset by Miramiska (Shutterstock)

Connect with Taylor García
Author website: www.btaylorgarcia.com

 @btaylorgarcia

First Edition

Printed in the United States of America.

For Bonita and my boys—thank you for letting me go to these worlds inside my head. Your loving support sustains my heart, mind, and soul.

Para mi familia, siempre

El que busca encuentra.
-Dicho

"You think it's the end,
But it's just the beginning."
-Bob Marley & The Wailers

PREFACE

AS FAR AS WE KNOW, our people have been in the state now known as New Mexico since the 1600's, when the region was called Santa Fé de Nuevo Mexico, a remote northern province of then New Spain. And by our people, I mean my family, the descendants of the mestizos of the region—the mixed blood offspring of the indigenous peoples of the Southwest and the first waves of Spanish immigrants from the interior of what would eventually be called the country of Mexico. These early agrarian settlers of New Mexico were neither Native American, purebred Spaniards, nor Mexican quite yet, however their cultural identity as racial hybrids would remain a constant, while their national identity would shift over time based on which flag flew over the land. New Mexico's status as a province of New Spain ended in 1821 as a result of Mexico's independence from Spain, making the area a Mexican territory up until 1848, when, by way of the Mexican-American War, the United States gained control of New Mexico.

Multi-generational New Mexicans such as I have therefore suffered from a centuries-long identity crisis. What are we exactly? One somewhat logical label is Neomexicano, a sub-identity within the larger Hispano heritage. As New Mexicans, we are, in effect, our own off-shoot of a people that are not quite Native American, Iberian European (i.e. Spanish), or Mexican, yet we are indeed a blend of all three. We are New Mexican the way other Latinos consider themselves Puerto Rican, Cuban, Colombian, and so on. And so goes my origin story, the one that creeps up every time I complete a demographic survey.

In Latin American/Hispanic culture, name is often a key indicator of who you are. Within my lineage, there is one anomaly amongst the entirety of Spanish surnames in the pedigree: Taylor, my real "sur"-namesake. My great-great grandfather was an English immigrant who found his way to the New Mexico and Colorado region around the time of the Civil War, where he met my great-great-grandmother Trujillo and started the Taylor family. On the other side of my family, one name has remained a constant since 1825: García. My great-great-great grandfather García was himself the essence of a simple Northern New Mexico farmer living in the heart of northern native New Mexico.

Who these men really were, my grandfather's Taylor and García, is mostly lost to history, but it is here, with their names combined to form my pen name as a means to honor my heritage, that I present this novel, the story of a Mexican man who immigrates to the United States—the other side. Although they are neighboring countries with a border that has historically caused more harm than good, Mexico and the United States are bound by land and history, with the foundation being the cultures and identities that often blend to form a hybrid all its own.

1 - DETAINEE

Otay Mesa Detention Center—San Diego County

TONIGHT, I CANNOT SLEEP.

Around me, is a sea of men—some sitting up, others laying, talking, whispering, laughing, snoring—each of us floating on a cot, two feet apart from each other, enclosed by a chain-linked fence. My slow breathing won't calm me, won't trick me into sleep and off to the world of dreams where I might find Joanne, the last person I was with—my last hope. Praying and begging to Our Lady for some rest feels useless.

The officers come through once, twice, and three times, shining and waving their torches over our bodies as though they're blessing us with holy water. The light splashes on our chests, heads, and eyes while the other men say, *"ais, ais, ais"* as a warning. After the officers' last pass through, the sea calms and the other men fell asleep. For me, still nothing.

I still feel cold even in my new orange suit with the word "DETAINEE" on the back. Some men have a blanket or a tin foil over them. I'm too new, and even though I'm older than most of the men here, there is no pity on me. Earlier, when I first arrived, the officers told me to strip the clothes Hugo López had given me the day before. They told me to pull down my underwear and squat so they could shine a light up me, but they didn't help me stand, not knowing how my knee and hip ache at my age.

The warehouse is both dark and light, and the only way I know it's morning is when the large lamps high above flicker on. Their brightness makes the room feel like a hospital in the middle of the night. With no windows, there is no sun, and with no sun, no life.

On the first morning, after a breakfast that consisted of an apple, a cold piece of sausage and a slice of white bread, I'm then assigned to work in the bathrooms. I learn that we can change jobs after a while, after the new detainees come in, and others leave. We can mop the floors, empty out the garbage, clean in the kitchen, or work outside. I was once told that those jobs are not easy to get. Just a few days ago, I was frying totopos at Sea of Cortez Mexifresh Cantina y Cocina. I pray I could go back there. I'd be happy to eat their salty black beans again.

My first day turns into another one, and another, and another. At this point, I've lost count because every day is exactly the same. The only difference is my body gets more tired and sore. I asked for a pad for my knees for when I scrubbed the floors and an agent said he would check, but that was a few days ago. At work, there are groups of us—four or five—each on a task. Everyone shares how long they've been here, and where they are in *the process*. The ones who have been here longer say which agents are more human than others, but they say almost all of them are evil in their own way. I realize I cannot listen only to these conversations. I must talk to the other detainees if I'm going to wake from this nightmare.

Sometimes, when it's quiet and when the agents have left, everyone stops working. I, however, keep scrubbing in between tiles. That's how everything feels—in between. *Purgatorio*. Not here, or there. Like Pablo from Joanne's book. Not dead or alive.

A young man I see every day comes closer to me, reminding me of my grown son because of his age. His features are different, he has a stronger jaw and working hands. Felipe took Teresa's round face, and her thinner frame.

We give each other quick head nods, to let each other know that we are people, and that we're not forgotten.

"Slow down," the young man says. "No one's watching."

He's already like a friend by the time we gather the mops, brushes, and cleaning solutions, before we march off to our stations.

"Osvaldo Reyes," I offer my hand.

"Marcos. Marcos Gomez," he says as he gives me a handshake. "How long has it been?"

"Don't know. Two or three weeks now?"

"It's easy to lose track," he says.

"You?"

"Nine months, I think," Marcos scratches his head.

"Nine months? Oh, my God. How did they get you?"

"I came here to keep my family safe. We left Honduras because of the violence and there wasn't work. My wife's brother was in a gang and terrorized the family. We tried to stay away, but he stole from their mother and threatened them. He wanted me to join, and I told him I didn't want to. I tried to stand up to him, but he pulled a knife on me. See."

Marcos pulls up his orange top, revealing a scar on his stomach.

"He wanted to kill me right then. He was crazy and high. He talked about killing my wife—his own sister—and our kids."

"It sounds like you have a good case to stay."

"There's too many of us. Most of us here are just like me. Young men trying to find a safe place to work and take care of our families."

"You can find work. There is work here."

"This country doesn't want us. They're telling us to turn back by ripping apart our families and sending people back without a trial. I don't know where my wife and our two children are. I have a boy and a girl, who are eight and nine—but they're gone."

"Sent back?"

"No. I don't know. Somewhere else, but not here." Marcos shudders and I pat his back.

He cries and doesn't hide it. Another man nearby, Gregorio, says he fled El Salvador with his wife and a toddler. They made it as far as Fresno with help from their relatives. Miguel, a single man also from Mexico, says he's been in for what has felt like a year. No one on either side of the border was concerned about him. No case, no attorney, just lost. It's true this country is the land of free, but only to those who pay their time in full.

3

"What about you, tío? How did you get caught?" Marcos wipes his eyes, then slaps my back. I feel the strength in his hand, and if he were to tunnel out of here, I might follow him.

"Expired visa. I knew someone in San Diego. A friend. But then an agent . . . it's not important." I trail off, not wanting to talk to anyone about it.

My apprehension was horrible. There I was, finally reunited with Joanne, and then one of the few people I knew in this town—one of the only people I trusted—young and sweet Daisy from Sea of Cortez was there to take me away.

"Don't worry, tío. I understand. They trap us like rats, but you're lucky. You had a visa and you're going to fly out of here. Find an attorney and plead your case. They should have pity on a hard worker like you. You and the white men. Watch how fast they come in and out of here. The system loves them. If you're young and brown, plan to stay. You're older, so maybe they'll take care of you. No offense, tío. They just don't want people like me."

"There's hope for all of us. Like the saying, hope dies last."

"You're an optimist," Marcos says, "That's good."

An officer comes back through our work area. Today we're scrubbing in the showers, the smell of Clorox burns my eyes and nose. Marcos, the other men, and I get back to work.

AFTER A FEW WEEKS, sleeping becomes easier. Drifting away on my cot, and after the voices hush, I think about my grandson, Estéban, my son Felipe, and my daughter-in-law, Ramona. They don't know I'm here. Felipe still thinks I'm working at the Faith Mission World Center as a teacher. He never knew about the last few weeks at the restaurant. As I think about them and pray for them, I worry I'll never see them again. Sometimes I wonder if this is finally my punishment for living the way I did. For my years as a zócalo boy, for the tiny faith I still held for Joanne, even when I was happily married. How I was given a good and strong marriage, a happy healthy son, and suffered no ailments or diseases like my father. I didn't die young like my mother, and I made enough money and had a decent life. But I was stained, and yes, perhaps all those gifts I received now had to be returned.

At work in the stalls, showers and toilets—there seems to be hundreds—I begin to tell Marcos about me, but in small pieces. He knows I'm sixty-five, from Oaxaca, and that I'm widowed. I mentioned Joanne once, then changed the subject because I needed to be careful about what I share and who I share it with. Or do I? Why does it matter now? I'm starting to fade away like everyone in here. When you're in this place, separated from your loved ones—you begin to die. My body aches are stronger now and my muscles are weaker. My heart seems to beat slower. Marcos says they pay us a few dollars a day, but I haven't seen a check, and even if I did, what would I do with it?

Some days, there are visitors. If you have a visitor, ICE comes, gets you and leads you away somewhere, but not for very long, maybe half an hour. Those who've had visitors say they were talking with their attorney or a relative. The ones with attorneys say you can't pay your way out, and that the attorney needs to fight it in court. Some get a court date and never return. I've heard those that get caught, like me, sometimes get sent back sooner than those asking permission like Marcos.

"It's all the same," Marcos says. "They decide what they want and when. La migra is working overtime. They're catching everyone."

There have been no visitors for me. No letters either. Some of the men get letters. The envelopes already torn open; the pages stuffed back inside. Some of them are from above the border and others from below, making the men weep, while others toss them aside.

Joanne would know what to do. She's smart. She knew what was happening. She saw it all. She could do something. She could be my visitor or not. She could have moved on and forgotten about everything, forgotten about me. Dear God, no. Blessed Mother, please no. Joanne is the only one that knows I'm here, just her and Daisy.

Without a good way to track the passage of time—or a reason to do it— my time inside feels like a never-ending month. Marcos says it's been at least three. The calendar in the agent break room where we sometimes clean now shows November with a few days marked off with a pink slash through the dates. I remember it was August when I came in. We joke that the agents control everything, including time. Their stone faces and how they talk to us with short, cold commands make it true. Marcos warned me about the ones that speak Spanish—mediogringos, he calls them. They look like us, but they are white men underneath. He said not to trust their Spanglish.

Today, we're at a garbage sorting station going through glass and cans. It's a new job they've brought in. I'm taking lids off of the glass jars, plastic bottles and throwing them in separate containers. We go from one bin to the next with the agents coming by more often, keeping us moving. They must have some new contract and now they need the slaves to make them more money. I like the variety, but after a while, it's hard to keep up. Marcos and the other men have no problem with it. They dance through it.

On our water break, an officer named Lovato sets down a jug of water and cups. One of the other men takes the jug, pours the water, and passes the cups. Marcos points to his own eyes and cocks his chin to Lovato.

Lovato paces around us, inspecting our work. He holds up two fingers and whistles to us like animals. Everyone stops working.

Marcos warns me with his eyes. Lovato doesn't look scary, he's thin and doesn't have arms as big as the other officers. However, I can tell that everyone here is intimidated by him.

Marcos comes up to me and whispers, "Careful with this one, watch what you say."

I agree and take a sip of water. I bend to pick up the jug and on my way up I feel a pinch deep inside the muscles of my hip. I wince, let out a small yelp, "Ay!" I don't want any attention.

"Are you okay, tío?" Marcos helps me stand.

"Feels like a tear in my leg or hip."

Lovato stops circling, "What's the problem?" his Spanish is good but practiced.

"I, I think I'm hurt." I can stand all the way up, but it's painful. I try to stretch, but that makes it worse.

"He needs to sit down," Marcos says.

"No, I'm fine. I can go back to work."

"Mind your business," Lovato says to Marcos.

Lovato grabs the jug of water, takes the cups.

"Two more hours," he says.

I shuffle back to the bins with Marcos's help. The pain is still there, and I can only stand up by holding tight to one of the containers.

"You need help," Marcos says.

"No, no, I'm fine. You said he was a bad one."

"You're hurt. You need to sit. Lovato!"

Lovato struts back. "What?"

"He needs to rest."

"I thought I told you to mind your business," Lovato says.

"Come on, he's an old man. Help him out."

Lovato, maybe not a fighter as one might think of larger men, transforms into another thing. He becomes sharper as if wings or fangs have come out. It's in his face and how he stiffens up, pushing himself into the circle of men around me. He lunges toward Marcos's face, spiting as he shouts at him in Spanish.

"This isn't your job, fucker. This is my job. Your job is to do the work we give you. Do you understand? Do you understand me?" He jabs his fingers into Marcos' chest.

"Come on," Marcos says, not fighting back.

"You don't tell me how to do my work, okay? Okay?" Lovato turns his head to his shoulder and radios for back up.

"No, please, I'm fine." Stretching my body up, the pain isn't as bad, but it's replaced by a shiver of fear.

"Fine, fine," Marcos backs away. "Leave him."

Lovato stands down, but he's still enraged. He wants to prove himself. "That's what I said. Now back to work, all of you. Back to work, viejo."

He sneers at me, the word dripping out of his mouth. It's one of those words in Spanish that can sound nice to begin with—the simple way of saying 'old'—but add a brutal twist, a drop of the lower jaw to emphasize the 'jo' sound. The word takes on a whole new meaning—that it's wrong, dirty to be old. I turn and stare back at my bin to reach in the glass jars, but I don't grab anything—I'm stopped by Marcos swiftly passing behind me.

"That's it," he says, rushing toward Lovato.

He jumps the officer, brings him to the ground. I turn as best I can, limp toward them, pushing through the pain, and try to pull Marcos off of Lovato. Lovato, like a cat, leaps to his feet, delivering punches and kicks to Marcos, but the young man holds on and he fights back. I reach for him again, but I'm pulled away, and begin to feel the air leaving me the same way it did when I was apprehended. I feel an embrace of arms, those of different officers, pulling me away, landing blows on me. One connects with my shoulder, my chest—again, I'm breathless. I lay still, don't fight back. They'll stop if you don't fight back. At least that's what I think.

THE NEXT MORNING, I wake up in the infirmary, and just like every corner of this place, it's freezing cold. They keep the air conditioning on all day and night, and the blankets are like paper sheets. The nurses wear jackets and they move to keep warm, their shoes squeak on the immaculate sparkling floors because of our work, the prisoners. But no, this is not a prison. Remember? It's a detention center. Just like Purgatory. Just like this infirmary. It's in between the misery back in the chain-linked sea, and one step closer to death. It's nicer here though, because it's like a miniature hospital. Almost better than the hospital where Felipe was born at in Oaxaca City, or where Teresa had to go several times before she died, and bigger than the small clinic at the Faith Mission World Center in San Diego.

The bed is not a cot and yet it's not a real hospital bed. They don't want anyone staying here very long. It's not comfortable for bruised ribs, shoulders or a sprained wrist. They say the leg pain is a strain that has to heal with time and exercise, that it's not related to the injuries—the ones they inflicted. The nurses and doctors have somehow ignored how those happened. Checking the bruises—looking but not touching—they say to take a couple of days to rest here, but how under this sheet in the cold?

Marcos is nearby. He looks worse and has been sleeping longer. He might be sedated with drugs because his face is purple and swollen. One arm is over his chest, hugging himself. He got it worse than me from Lovato. Lovato had pity on me, the viejo. It was the other officers that didn't. Marcos wakes up at last and his puffy eyelids blink open.

"I told you, eh?" he says. "Watch out for those ones."

"You shouldn't have attacked him."

"He needed it."

"You're crazy and you're never getting out of here like that."

"I'm just trying to get out faster."

"Thank you for defending me."

"You need it, tío," Marcos says. "Who's going to take care of you?"

"You know, I have a son, maybe a little bit older than you."

"Can't he get you out?"

"He doesn't know I'm here. No one does."

"I think everyone forgot about me, too," he says.

"You'll get out. I've been praying for you."

"You know that's all for nothing, right? You know all of this is? You know it doesn't matter what happens. Nothing matters, tío. Nothing."

He tries to sit up but can't. His face twists up with pain.

"Stop talking like that. This will be over someday."

"That's it, tío. Might be over someday next week, next month, or even next year. Who knows? And you know what, that little Officer Lovato, they're not going to do anything to him. He'll get an award for what he did to us."

"They said you can make complaints."

"This isn't a hotel." Marcos closes his eyes, pretends to sleep. "Nothing matters."

A nurse comes in to check on us. She goes to Marcos first, checks his breathing, and his bandages. She feels his forehead for a temperature. She looks kind, like she shouldn't be working in a place like this, but since she is, she might be one of the good ones.

She comes over to me. "Are you feeling okay?"

"What time is it? How long have I been here?"

"It's seven in the morning. You two have been asleep all night. Did he hurt you?"

"Yes, it hurts. But I'll be fine."

"We've heard he's a bad one." She looks back at Marcos.

"Who? Him? No, he didn't hurt me. It was Lovato, the ICE agent. He hurt us both."

"Lovato?"

"Yes, it's a lie if they told you he hurt me. Marcos is my—he's like a son to me."

"Lovato did this?" she asks again, her Spanish turning to English.

"Yes, I'm telling you the truth. He's a bad man."

The nurse shakes her head, turns to Marcos.

"When he wakes up, we need to talk to him."

An ICE agent walks in, looks around. "Nurse Vargas?" he says.

"Yes?"

"Here, this is for one of them."

He hands her a thick brown envelope stuffed with papers and is gone as soon as he came.

"You're Osvaldo Reyes, right? T93524?" She reads from the envelope.

"Yes."

It's been through many hands, the flap ripped open, whatever is inside was already handled—beaten up and shoved back in, like us. It's warm though, like a heart still beating. There's life in it, and it's the only real thing I've seen in a long time.

"Thank you, Nurse Vargas."

"Call me Yolanda. Please rest. Thank you for telling me about Lovato. That's—terrible," she says, and squeaks out.

The writing on the front is Joanne's. Her handwriting, so perfect and even, how it leans backward, trying not to be a bother. Or could this be nothing? A mistake, meant for another Osvaldo Reyes. Or even if it is from her, does it matter, like Marcos says? Does anything matter?

Marcos flutters his eyes open, "What is it, tío?"

I reach inside and pull out a small card with a picture of a palm leaf leaning over a clear pond, the tip of the leaf touching the water, making ripples. It's hope and sympathy blending together all at once.

"It's from her. She found me."

"What does it say?"

Dear Osvaldo,

I don't know if you will get this. I hope you do. It has taken me a while to find where to send this, to see if you are there. They won't let me talk to you. I can't call. If you are there, I need to know. I need to visit you and tell you how I will get you out. I hope you are safe and healthy. I am so sorry for what happened to you. I felt helpless when they ripped you away like an animal. I've been thinking of you every day and wanted to send you what they stole from you. It meant so much to me that you still had my original copy that I had written so long ago. I hope it brings you comfort until we get you out. The system is so complicated, and I don't even know where to begin, but know I'm going to try my best. Write back to this address and let me know if you received this.

Missing you,

Joanne

My stomach twists as I feel the thickness of the same book I had been carrying with me since I left Mexico months ago.

"See," Marcos says. "I told you'd get out."

"It's just a letter."

"From your lover." He smiles. "What's all the paper?"

"It's nothing, it's just . . . and she isn't my—"

"She loves you. Who is she? Is she getting you out? You know, tío, you haven't told me much about yourself. What is your story anyway?"

I close the card and slide it under my hurt leg. I squeeze the stack of white typed paper, hugging my hands around it and feeling happy to be reunited with it.

Marcos, his face beaten, his body abused—we're in the same position. Brothers in a larger hemisphere, trapped in time. I want him to know. I want someone to know who I am.

"Well, then I'll tell you. I'll tell you everything."

2 - TERESA

"MY WIFE, TERESA, PASSED AWAY, almost two years ago. I believe I mentioned that to you. We were married forty years. We had one son together. Felipe, who's about your age. He's a grown man now, has his own son—my grandson, Estéban. Teresa and I were a happy couple. We met where we worked."

"Where was that?"

"In Oaxaca City there is a school called El Instituto Cultural de Oaxaca. It's a language school, mostly for adult tourists. They come to learn Spanish and how to cook. Make crafts. I was an art instructor, and I taught people how to make pottery."

"You were a teacher?"

"Yes, and so was Teresa. She was the cooking instructor. All the men signed up for her class so they could get a free meal at the end of the day, so she says. I think it was because Teresa was young and beautiful. She was also serious. She seemed tough on the outside. And she wore glasses. This intimidates some men. And fascinates them, too. I liked everything about her. I had never met a woman like her. When I took the job there at the Instituto, I sat behind her during one of my first staff meetings. She was taking notes and watching the principal speak. Teresa brushed a strand of her dark hair behind her ear, and she turned to me, probably felt me starting, and then gave me an expression that said, 'What are you looking at?' I was studying the hand she lifted up to fix her hair—her ring finger. She was single."

"A lover from the beginning," Marcos says.

"I knew something about women."

"Ay, get on with it, old man."

"It wasn't a romance from the beginning, though. She was quiet and reserved. And we went slow with it. Very slow. The Instituto was like a hacienda, rooms on the perimeter and a large garden in the center. This was covered in grass, and it was where students met in between classes or sat in the afternoon. We teachers would see each other all day passing under the arched walkways. The art shop was close to the kitchen and there I would see Teresa come out to meet her students. She denied it, but we began making eyes at each other then. A small side peek or a glance over the shoulder. That was all it was for a long time."

"You never talked or asked her out?"

"Yes, but that was later. We were growing something little by little. It was nice to have a slow relationship like that. It was what I preferred."

"What do you mean?"

"I'll explain. First, I'll tell you when the romance really began. One late August afternoon, when all of her students had gone home for the day, she had, at last, invited me over. In the kitchen that day, they had made tamales and mole and there was a lot left over. The wide dining room connected to the kitchen covered in tiles with blue sparrows smelled of wet ground corn, and the scent of the fresh husks still lingered. The strong smell of chocolate and chile made it feel like the mole had come to life. I'm starving just thinking about it."

"Me, too," Marcos says.

"'There's so much food,' she said. 'Will you make a plate?'

"I served myself and sat at the long table where Teresa's students prepared and ate each afternoon, learning how to grind corn, mix champurrado, or wrap tamales. She went back to work clearing the stove, putting pots and plates in the sink to soak. I felt like I knew her already. Being in her kitchen was like being home.

"She wiped her hands on a towel at her waist and tilted her head when she looked at me.

14

"'How are they?' The strand of hair she always tucked behind her ear fell in front of her cheek again.

"'Make a plate, too,' I said, 'and come sit with me in the patio. I can't eat this delicious food alone.'

"She hesitated, put her hand on her stomach, but I held her gaze, said to her with my eyes that I would wait. I had learned that's what a man must do for the woman he honors. He will wait for her every move. For her to sleep, bathe, get dressed and ready, for her to take the first bite of her meal. He will wait.

"As I waited for her, I knew she was unlike any other woman. With Teresa, I saw something else. Something new. A safe place at last. I never felt I had to pretend to be someone else with her."

"So you felt that way with other women?" Marcos says.

"Yes, but Teresa was different. She fixed a plate and we moved out to the patio. The school was quiet except for traffic on Niños Héroes on the other side of the tall adobe walls. We kept quiet eating and stole those little glances of each other in the afternoon light. She smiled. I smiled back. Then I asked her if she would want to meet one day outside of the school. She took a bite, swallowed. Waited for me, made we wait, then she said yes.

"The rest was, well, our love story. We spent every day together at work, then at home. She in the kitchen at the Instituto with the women, often single travelers, or the other halves of a couple, or those hungry men looking for free food. Over in the art shop, I had most of the men and the younger students that needed to be doing something with their hands. Clay calmed them all. Every student went home with a small cup, the easiest thing to make.

"Even until our last few years working at the Instituto together, our relationship flourished, growing in a sweet silence as we acknowledged each other as coworkers—teachers in the same school—at a distance, separated by an expansive lawn—a miniature paradise. We would send each other small nods or the rare wink, maybe a quick signal about another teacher or some student gossip, they were all just ways to keep the game going we had made up—that we were secret lovers, two lonely teachers that had fallen in love. But everyone knew Osvaldo and Teresa were exactly what we were: lifelong novios—the heart and soul of the Instituto Cultural de Oaxaca."

"How you talk, man. Like a poet. This is perfect. You were blessed."

"I believe I was. But I also believe I paid for my ways. What I haven't told you is who I was before Teresa."

Marcos tries to sit up. He winces as he turns to me. He's waiting to hear it.

"We were still young. Felipe was a boy. We were clearing out our storage and throwing things away, donating old clothes and houseware to our friends and family. We needed space for our work tools, her pots and pans, my clay and spinning tables. She came across a box I hadn't touched in years. A hatbox where I had put old cards and pictures. Teresa dusted it off, opened it, and as her hands lifted the top off, my stomach fell remembering what was inside. Letters from a woman—the first woman I loved. There was a strip of photos in there, too, me and Jo—the woman—in a picture booth. Underneath it was this right here. This stack of papers. It's a small book Joanne wrote. I don't know why I kept them all. I guess I thought one day I might find her again, but time went forward, and I hid them away and forgot about them. Teresa looked at them. 'What are these?,' she asked. 'Nothing, nothing,' I said, but nothing means something. She shuffled through them and just shook her head, threw the box on the floor, and walked away."

"The letters, they were from her—Joanne?" Marcos points to the envelope on my lap.

"Yes. From Joanne. The woman I know here in the United States. Joanne was my first real girlfriend, if you can call her that, before I knew Teresa. I was younger and—I went the wrong way. When we met, I was—I can't—"

"Go on, tío. We have time."

In the solitude of the infirmary, the day still young, I decide to share my dark secret with Marcos.

"I met Joanne when I worked on the streets. I was a zócalo boy. Do you know what that is?"

"You walked the zócalo begging for money?"

"Well, yes, but in exchange for . . . services. Language lessons, tours." I hesitate to say it. "Companionship."

"Companionship?"

"Yes, that kind."

"Joanne was your . . . client?"

"Well, no. We never—you see, we became friends."

"And Teresa? Did she know about you working the streets?"

"I told her. Eventually. I had to tell her the truth, when I explained who Joanne was."

"Did Teresa kick you out?"

"She was hurt, of course. She said, 'Are you still in love with this woman?'"

"No, I said to her. No. She had a harder time with what I once did on the zócalo, but I told her everything, how it all started and when it ended, how it ended with Joanne, how Joanne was my last and that I never went back to it. That's when I decided I wanted to be a teacher. Over time, she understood, or at least I think she did. She seemed to build a certain denial about anything that happened before we came together and married, and with that, I believed she had put away any thought about my past as a zócalo boy.

"But when the words *love letters*, or *prostituta* were said in other passing conversations, in stories told by other people, or on television or in a movie, they hit me in the gut, and I wondered if those words bothered her too. Did she feel my pang of guilt each time? Did she think for a moment, 'What have I done?' You never know. You never know what goes on in someone's head. In marriage, you shouldn't try to, or you will go crazy. You let go of the past so that you can move forward together. The marks and scars remain, but you don't keep looking at them.

"Love returned. We kept our passion alive. We had to for Felipe. We tried for more children but never had anymore. Maybe that was the scar. We grew older and slower, the displays of our romance changed into making the other person a cup of tea or folding all the laundry, letting one sleep late, or putting away all the groceries. And thanking the other for everything. That's also what happens in marriage. You begin as strangers, transform into lovers, then grow into friends.

17

"The lovemaking stopped when Teresa's cancer arrived. We tried one last time on our anniversary, the summer before she died. Afterward, we held each other, and she ran her hands through the hair that was left on the sides of my head. She smiled and kissed my cheek and forehead.

"'You are such a good man,' she said. 'You have been so good to me.'

"That last year tested us. The doctors said it had spread from her breast to her lungs and that there was not much to do to stop it. Felipe and Ramona were going to pay to send us to Mexico City to a treatment center, but Teresa said no. She said she felt most comfortable at home. I took care of her, cooked, cleaned, took her to the doctor for her therapy. Felipe and Ramona helped, too. It's what Teresa wanted, to be with her family. In that year, we made one trip to the coast, to the hills of Puerto Escondido to see my madrina Adelina. Adelina was a curandera and I believe she helped Teresa live longer.

"In bed naked with Teresa, her body smaller and weaker, her once thick hair in patchy whips, I held her and said, 'Tell me everything,' I said. 'Tell me your fears, your dreams.'

"'You know everything already.'

"I was silly to think that I should have forgiveness for the two times I ruined her, one with the truth of what I once was, and two for keeping it from her. Why dig up the past? She gazed into my eyes and smiled too weak to revisit the painful times. And why would she want to? It was so selfish for me to think I had room on her deathbed."

"And then you came here to the U.S. to start over? Just like that?"

"There's more to the story. There always is, carnal."

3 - SABBATICAL

"IN HER FINAL DAYS, WHEN THERE wasn't much left of her, we held on
to each other. Felipe and his family kept their vigil too. Estéban came to kiss
his grandma and hold her hand. Teresa looked at all of us, then turned to me
and said to keep on living. When it was just the two of us, she said to me,
'Go see the world while you can. Don't wait for me.' No, no, I said to her. I
need you. She gave a weak smile, her eyes brightened one last time. 'There's
a lot of life in you yet. Live. Don't be alone. You have my permission.'

"Once death indeed parts, what happens next is the unknown. Felipe and
I filled the holes in our hearts with each other's company. We clung to one
other for months. He and Ramona made a room for me to stay on those nights
when I lingered after dinner, when Estéban stayed on my lap as we watched
TV. Ramona kept giving me cups of chocolate, or Felipe and I would drink
a beer, and then another, and sometimes another while we played dominoes.
One time the little bastard wanted to bring out the mezcal. Could you imagine
how mad Teresa would have been seeing her husband and son getting drunk
on mezcal trying to feel better? But that was how it was those first few tender
months. It's how someone fights loneliness. No man, no matter how strong,
can make sense of losing the most important woman in his life.

"I continued to work at the Instituto, though the memories of Teresa were
stronger there. The two of us grew up there together, and the history of it all
stared back at me with more intensity through the eyes of our work family.
How they consoled me, brought me cards and gifts. They mourned for
Teresa, too. I had to tell Soledad, Teresa's fellow teacher in the kitchen, no

after a while—she always invited me in for lunch or to stay for dinner with the last afternoon class—she was only being nice—but the smells of cooking oil and coffee, simple things like an apron or a potholder Teresa had used, prevented me from going further than the doorway. Soledad understood after some time and left plates wrapped in foil for me in my workshop. I took them home and ate the food alone, then brought the plates back to my shop, too much of a baby to bring them back to the school kitchen myself.

"And the students knew it, too. Osvaldo and Teresa were a package. One could take pottery with el señor and cooking with la señora. For almost a year there, the students arrived to find my other half missing and so began their own mourning. One day my principal, Señora Topete, suggested a sabbatical. Some teachers had taken these mysterious things—these long intellectual journeys—vacations, really. Some returned with more stories and culture, new plans, new ideas, a new look. Others never returned. I had the impression Señora Topete was suggesting the second plan. 'Take as much time as you need,' she had said.

"It felt much like that permission Teresa had given me, though Teresa's permission, I had wondered, might have been for me to be with others. No wife would say, 'After I die, go find another woman as soon as you can,' yet she could suggest not to be alone, as Teresa did. For a time there, I thought Soledad might have been trying to talk to me, and maybe once or twice I had thought about taking her offer to stay in the kitchen to eat with her. I was missing that simple companionship with a woman, and maybe Soledad knew that.

"And yet, I felt watched, not by Teresa's spirit, but by guilt, either mine or of that around me. Ramona, my daughter-in-law, had lost an aunt around that time—they were friends of ours—and Ramona's uncle Jaime seemed to have wasted no time at all bringing another woman around to gatherings and even to another funeral of a more distant relative, or so I heard from my son. Ramona's family separated into two groups: those in favor of Tío Jaime going on living, and those who thought Tía Ysabel needed more rest in her grave—at least several years—before Jaime went around like a man whore.

"And there it was. That idea of who—of what I was. If I were to even entertain the idea of sitting to have a meal with another woman, I risked repeating history, or of tempting the devil. Not that I was going to go around the zócalo again looking for clients—imagine: an old man like me prowling like that—but how and when could I begin to start over with someone else? How and when would it feel normal to be with someone other than Teresa?

"That I felt that way was a sign that the clouds were lifting. I still mourned Teresa, still missed her with all of my soul, but I found a way to live in the new world. The loneliness in our home became a companion itself. With no one watching I felt more at ease. It was then the memories of Joanne returned. She began creeping into my thoughts now and again— just quick flashes of those times together when we were young—ideas I brushed away and tried to forget. Then, the memories that had grown hazy over time began to come back into focus. The gaps had filled in. She came to me in those early morning hours, when I was still asleep but coming to life, when all the dreaming souls return to their bodies after wandering all night. Or she'd come back to me in an instant out of nowhere, when I walked the zócalo in the early evening, or if I saw a tourist at the Instituto that looked like a younger version of her, working their clay in my class, trying to hide in plain sight.

"That spring I trained a new potter to work as my substitute. He was an eager young man and as the time approached for my official last day, I realized that I would not be returning to the Instituto. They were making way for me to retire. Señora Topete wanted to give a party for all the teachers and students, but I said no, and so we settled for a small gathering over coffee and panes in the courtyard after the students had gone home.

"That day, I came home with all of my pieces that sat on the shelves in my workshop. Some were rough, others painted and glazed a deep blue. That was the color I used the most. There were matching slender toothbrush holders, soap dishes, coffee mugs, plates, fruit bowls, garlic keepers, spoon rests, tortilla warmers, ashtrays, and more vases than anyone needed. Each of them with my initials etched into the bottom. I had experimented with intertwining them to be more artistic, the R for Reyes diagonal to the O for Osvaldo, the R inside it, the O by itself; none were as authentic as O and R, side by side. OR. Teresa and I used a small cup I had made that was too shallow to drink from, a dish more than anything, for our wedding rings. It was where I placed her band after she passed away.

"Bringing my pieces home felt like the true ending. I had offered them to the new instructor, suggesting he could give them away to the students as souvenirs of Sr. Reyes. No, he said, with a happy young smile. We'll make new ones. At home I put them in our storage. In there, I found it again. The box. The cursed box. In the days after Teresa found it, I suppose I never got around to purging it. It must have gotten kicked back in or under something, finding it's place and waiting for me at that exact moment.

"I brought the box inside and spent more time with it than I should have. I re-read Joanne's letters, and studied the photo strip we had taken in Ensenada the last time we saw each other. I remembered we had cut the strip in half. She kept the first two frames, and I kept the last two. In those ones, Joanne stared into me, her hand placed lightly on my cheek. In the last image, our faces connected like a puzzle, my jutting nose and solid round jaw pressed onto the half-moon of her light skin. Her eyes were closed, and her lips touched mine.

"After reading the letters, which were like a drug, I began to read the book she wrote. It was about a man who could travel outside of his body when he slept. She said she based the main character on me. That's what this is."

"Have you read it?" Marcos asks.

"Yes, a few times. My curiosity about her letters and the book made me want to try to find her. What harm could it do, I thought?

"Teresa and I never fooled with computers. We didn't own one, and when the Instituto started asking us to enter our notes into two new ones they had brought to the teachers' workroom, I rarely brought myself to use it. My son, Felipe, however, spent a lot of time on his at home. He and Ramona had their own lives on them it seemed. There and on their phones. I never bothered, but I knew that if I were to try to find Joanne again, I would need to stare into that screen and search.

"It felt wrong and foreign at first, then it scared me how easy it came. How you simply typed into the open box and thousands of results came back. I didn't go searching for Joanne Watson immediately. Instead I looked at things near her. United States. California. Southern California. San Diego. San Diego State University. That's where she was going to go for more schooling when I met her. Felipe asked about what I was looking up.

"'We have distant relatives in Los Angeles,' I said. 'I thought I might find them, then stay in the United States for a while. Maybe find work there.'

Felipe was terrified at first.

"'Why would a man your age want to go to the United States,' he said. 'You know it's not the place it once was? Its arms are no longer open.'"

"'It would only be for a few months,' I told him.

"'They treat immigrants and refugees like animals now, you know?' he said."

"'Help me, son. Your mother wanted me to keep living. She said so.'

"Felipe almost fell apart. I thought he might cry or hit me for what I had said. I don't know what the future holds, I said. I have to create one.

"I would not say I had his blessing, but he did understand after a while. I believe he realized then that I still had life in me. It had been almost a year. Teresa was well at peace and though my heart was broken, it didn't seem that I was going to follow Teresa to the grave just yet.

"And so, the real search began. When Felipe wasn't looking, I finally typed it in. Joanne Watson. I imagined she had married, had a different last name. Maybe nothing would come back. Nothing did. Just names and faces of other women named Joanne Watson. I remembered how Felipe searched on the computer. How he typed in many words into the box. I tried, *Joanne Watson Michigan*. Where she was from. *Joanne Watson California. Joanne Watson San Diego. Joanne Watson San Diego State University.*

Then a picture appeared. It was her. She was smiling. I remembered her smile like it was yesterday. How her eyes held a secret. In the picture, she was standing with a group of women. It looked like they had received an award. I read her name in the caption below. Joanne Watson McCasey. English Faculty. Her dream to teach had come true. Did she publish her book? I didn't find anything about that yet. And yes, it was certain she had married because of the second last name. I typed and clicked further and found an image of a man I thought was her husband. A man with the last name McCasey. He was standing in front of a religious center in San Diego. The Faith Mission World Center. Maybe Joanne had found God, I thought.

I clicked. Clicked again. And again. I watched her lifetime flash before me. She had her own page with lists of accomplishments, degrees, and titles. She looked secure and important and smart as always. She was a fully grown adult, not the timid girl I remembered walking around the zócalo.

"How amazing you found her," Marcos said.

"I admit I felt like a spy snooping around like that."

"Again with your guilt, tío," Marcos said. "You were only following your instincts. You're a human. There's nothing wrong with that."

"That's the problem. The battle between the heart and the head."

4 - ZOCALO BOY

"WAIT, TÍO. ABOUT YOUR DAYS ON the zócalo. How? Why?" Marcos says.

"Like I said, I'm too ashamed to say."

"Don't worry, tío. I won't judge you."

Cold air blasts into the room, cooling us and not in a good way. Marcos coughs, his face twists up in pain.

"Let's call the nurse. You need more pain medicine."

"No, tío. I don't want their drugs. Keep talking."

"Well, it all started with sugar."

"Sugar?"

"Growing up, our home was full of sweets. All of our cupboards, and closets, and the narrow hallway from my parents' bedroom to mine and my sister's room was stacked with tamarindos, cajetas, chicles—everything in bright wrappers—loomed over us, teased us. It was forbidden for us to touch it or even think about it. The only place we were allowed to handle them was in the zócalo, where my Papá sold them from a small table he set out every morning under a laurel tree. He would give us a few to go peddle to people walking by, and he made sure to keep count and check our pockets. Each piece, he said, meant money. Food on our table. He said to separate yourself from them—see them as a means to an end. This helped with the sex work later, the removal of myself as a way of protection.

"We competed with so many children in the zócalo, like the little indigenous children and their mothers holding their candy, selling only a few pieces a day so they might go buy something from the market that night. I felt guilty for all the candy we had at home, how my father dressed us and said to charm the tourists. He was a master at work. He knew Spanish, of course, Zapotec, Mazateco, a little French, German and English. He could speak to anyone. He demonstrated how to be patient, how to stall someone and tempt them, how to take a refusal, and then turn it into a sale. He started selling comic books, too. He dreamed of opening his own permanent kiosk where we would sell magazines, cigarettes, and toys.

"We didn't make much, but when we came home with money every day, we felt rich. We turned in our centavos to Papá and he put them away. Mamá, however, made more money. She was a housekeeper and a washerwoman. She worked so hard. Harder than my father, and she only made it known in how she groaned at the end of her workdays, standing in our tiny kitchen turning masa into tortillas, warming them on the hot comal and feeding us when she was exhausted. Though her physical labor made her body sturdy, I believe to this day it was what made her die first. I never thought she would, and it occurred to me that when Teresa passed before me, maybe I hadn't worked as hard, that maybe I protected my body too much. Again, the guilt I felt.

"But that was later in life. Mamá was forced to work even harder when Papá became sick. One winter, he caught a flu that turned into pneumonia. He kept standing out in the zócalo only making his illness worse. After that, he was never the same. He couldn't breathe normally anymore. So what did he do? He stayed inside and started to eat the candy. We stopped selling it too because we weren't cute kids anymore begging tourists. As my father gained weight from the sugar, he developed diabetes. It was common to see him lying on his back on the couch, listening to the television, sleeping off and on, waking to cough, and we running to him to make sure he was still breathing.

"It was in those days when my Tío Miguel Angel sat and talked with my father. Miguel Ángel was only twenty-four, but he seemed older, and he wanted to be called tío, even though he was Papá's cousin. With lighter skin, thin lips, and wavy hair, they sometimes called Miguel Ángel pretty, and it was no secret what he did for work.

"'Oaxaca is being discovered,' he said. 'More tourists than ever before are arriving, and from everywhere. They want to *feel* the culture, and they have money to spend doing it.'

"Miguel Ángel had transformed from a city laborer to a dandy helping these eager visitors learn about the city. He came like a messenger to Papá.

"'Take Osvaldo out,' Papá had said unable to move himself, the diabetes slowly killing his lower limbs. 'He knows how to sell sugar.'

"'But this isn't selling gum, primo,' Miguel Ángel had said to my father.

"'He'll take care of himself, won't you, Valdo?' my father had said.

"SO, MY FIRST TIME WAS a late July evening, when Miguel Ángel led the cruise around the zócalo. He had picked my clothes: pressed slacks of his that hung too big on my narrow hips, and a white collared shirt.

"It was busy that night, ciudadanos and tourists making laps, mariachis tuning their violins and plucking their guitarrónes waiting for a request, and a payaso wearing big blue pants, his face painted white and pink around the lips, pantomiming for a growing crowd. Standing around the low walled tree beds, a few with one foot resting up on the concrete, others with their hands in their pockets, eyes expectant like street dogs, were the other young men of the trade.

"They had blended in at first glance, then came into clear view, sizing up their new competition. For me, a newly turned seventeen-year-old virgin, this once safe and comforting open garden—a harbor for families, children, festivals—felt exposed, the insides pulled out and on display for only adults to see.

"'The job's not hard,' Miguel Ángel had said. 'You work as much as you want, and you make it what you want. See there? That one wants a little history. That one, language lessons. And that one? You see her, Valdito? She wants a boyfriend for the week. And she's got a little money, too. Can't you tell? That's the one you want. Come on. Let's walk by her.'

"The woman sat alone, sipping a large margarita under a crisscross of small light bulbs on a raised patio. The afternoon rain had kept the air thick with humidity into the evening, cooled only by the rustle of the laurel trees.

"'It's her first night here,' Miguel Ángel whispered. 'Watch me.'

"'E'cuse me, señorita?' Miguel Ángel held up his finger and rested his other hand on the railing. 'The best margaritas in town are there.' He pointed up over his shoulder. 'Teranova.'

"'Oh, really?' she said. Late thirties, Miguel Ángel had predicted. Americana with curves. Her brown, freshly styled hair rested on her shoulders. 'I think this one's pretty good.'

"'Having dinner?' Miguel Ángel said.

"'No, not yet.' She tapped the table. 'Are you going to tell me where I should go eat?'

"'No,' He smiled. 'You're at the right place.'

"'So, I need to go there for drinks and here for dinner?' She leaned forward, rested her chin on clasped hands.

"'Here in México, we take our time,' he smiled at her. 'You tell me you need help here, okay? I show you around. We show you around.' He threw his arm around me, and I gave her a smile of my crooked teeth I still hide today.

"'Tour guides are you?' she said.

"'Better.' Miguel Ángel set his foot on the raised platform and pulled himself up to her level to shake her hand. 'Victoriano. A su servicio,' flashing his eyes at her. I could almost feel how he lit up for her, how he turned on his charm.

"'And you are?' she said to me.

"Before our stroll that night, Tío Miguel Ángel had said to create a fake name.

"'Never give your real name to someone you're going to sleep with,' he had said.

"I didn't know what to say. I hadn't given it a thought being so nervous about everything else. My real name, Osvaldo, had almost slipped out. 'Juan,' I said.

"'Why not, Rogelio, or Rosalio, or Rosendo?' he had teased nights later, when the evening walk was becoming a routine.

"The lady stood, extended her hand.

"'It's nice to meet you. Won't you two join me?'

"'I have another appointment,' Miguel Ángel said.

"'An appointment? It's eight o'clock at night,' she said.

"'You are in good hands with my friend Juan here.'

"Miguel Ángel patted me quickly on the behind, whispered under his breath, *'she's flirting with you, carnal, do it.'* I always wondered if Miguel Ángel took all clients, like some of the other zócalo boys. It was his main job, and he made a lot of money. It was quite possible, always saying how busy he was, going on trips to Huatulco and Puerto Escondido, but never saying with whom. Whether it was years or minutes ahead, I knew I could not think about the future. But I knew that my shame would not keep me in the business forever.

"'Kathy Richards, Houston, Texas,' the lady smiled and waved me over. 'Come sit.'

"Miguel Ángel nodded once, giving me the slightest wink, then moved on into the night.

"Kathy asked for help with the menu, what certain words were, how to say things in Spanish. She laughed and smiled, moved her bare shoulders to the music of the mariachis as they sauntered by. It was all like Miguel Ángel had said, it was so easy and innocent. She ordered an extra plate for me and shared her margarita. She ordered another one, pushing it toward me. As the night went on, she moved closer to me. She glanced at her watch, stretched her arms outward, dropping a hand on my knee.

"'Tengo—lo siento—I'm so tired,' she sighed. 'Will you walk me back to my hotel?'

"We were the same height, but I felt so small walking next to her. She was pretty and full of life, and it felt like those sweet dates—I had only had a few— where I brought a girl from either church or school with me to walk around, how we would find each other's hands, maybe find a corner out of sight to kiss. But I realized when I followed Kathy to her hotel, how she whispered to be quiet when she found her key outside of the locked door under the amber lamp, that this was going to be more than kissing on the street. Later, in her room, she said to wait while she went to the bathroom. She emerged in purple underwear, and sat on the bed, patting it. I clenched my fists to try to stop shaking.

"'How old are you?' she said, smiling.

"Miguel Ángel said to answer questions with other questions.

"'How old are you?'

"'You should know better to ask a lady's age.' Her lips turned flat.

"'I'm sorry, I'm sorry.'

"'No, no, no. Come here,' she said. 'Are you trembling? Is it cold in here?'

"I sat next to her, and she laid one hand on my leg. With her other one, she felt my face, ran her hand along my jaw. She caressed my thigh with her fingers, each pass moving closer and closer to the center of my body. The room went silent, and what happened next flashed by, each movement a snap of light with the smallest sounds like moths hitting a lightbulb. Clothes on skin, clothes off, skin pressing into skin, the slightest sweat of our two bodies mixing together. She stopped and said, 'You need to put something on.'

"She reached into the side table and gave me a condom. After a moment of my fumbling, she helped to put it on me with quick hands, like putting shoes on a child. I didn't know what was right or wrong, was it too fast or two slow, or whether I was supposed to feel anything—if I was allowed to.

"Afterward, Kathy stood, brought her underwear with her to the bathroom. She returned in a towel covering her body, the shower now running. She opened the small drawer again and pulled money out. For a moment there, I could see she didn't know how much—I had never said anything—and so she set a $500 peso bill face down, the Aztec sun stone shining up at me. My reward.

"'We might have to do that again.' She turned back to me, returning to the bathroom. 'Oh, I'm thirty-six,' she said. 'And it's okay. I'm divorced.'"

MARCOS SITS UP, SHAKES his head in disbelief.

"Don't mess with me, old man, are you serious?"

"Calm down, boy. It's not pornography."

"But that's—that's what you did. You really did that."

"That was the beginning."

"And seventeen-years-old," Marcos whistles. "That's why she wanted you."

"Stop it. She didn't know how old I was."

"Tell me more," Marcos says.

"See, that's why I don't want to talk about it. Men are disgusting. We think it's a treat to be a prostitute."

"I'm sorry, tío. I'm sorry. It was a—good story."

"You need sex. You're young."

"So then you kept doing that?"

"I had to. I had to make money for my family."

"And they supported it?"

"They ignored it. My mamá hated the idea of her son walking the streets to ask tourists if they needed help. Taking their money for some language lessons over a dinner they were going to pay for? Bah. At least that's what she told herself about what I was doing. If she had any idea about the sex, she denied it, but she knew Miguel Ángel, and that he wasn't just touring families around the town. She had seen all the new visitors he spoke of. Gringos, foreigners, women, lots of them. What was next? It was no different from las prostitútas, las putas, she said. She didn't like it, but she looked the other way. We needed the money. 'Take care of yourself,' she said. 'Don't lose yourself.' She had no idea.

"And after a while, it became normal. But I was cautious. I stuck with Tío Miguel most of the time. Sometimes we walked with the other groups of men, but we mostly stayed to ourselves. The groups of the other boys weren't big. Four, five at the most, in each pack. They kept a fair distance from each other, groups stationed at the corners of the plaza, under archways, around the trees. They stood around like they were friends enjoying the evening. The groups kept to their corners, switching places once in a while, and there was a definite order to getting the business, so no one was left out. It was like a restaurant, Miguel Ángel would say. Each new customer gets their own new waiter. Doesn't matter where those customers come in, though. Just as long as each boy moves forward at least once. It's up to you to catch and release.

"Because we traveled as a pair, we were less threatening, and could mix in with the other packs if we needed or wanted to. And because I was much younger and Miguel Ángel was older, the rest of the boys let us come and go with them, as though we balanced each other out. We still stayed in order though. No cheating there. Miguel Ángel liked to talk with other boys and share stories and successes and horrors, and he laughed with them, but I didn't. I kept to myself and became the one they made fun of. They called me fino. Too fine.

"I eventually chose to walk alone most of the time, and Miguel Ángel warned me that made women nervous. 'Who wants to talk to a man by himself,' he said. You have to joke around with the guys and act like you're talking about something mischievous and important that the women need to know. Your mood is contagious. When you're happy, they're happy. And they spend more money.

"Where many of the boys' specialty was dinner and dancing—this was better for business anyway, because it meant you were more likely to get into a bed that same night—I was best at strolling and sightseeing. Daytime work. I didn't have sex with every woman.

"'You'll be a vampire soon,' Miguel Ángel teased. 'You've already done it with a few, why not just do it with all of them?'

"I wanted to say, 'because not all of them want it,' but I didn't. I knew what he would say back to me. He would cut me down, remind that it was better than washing dishes in a restaurant or picking up trash or working in the fields. At least you're eating and having sex, he would say.

"My plan had always been to save up and go to school. I couldn't do that to my body and think it would be good for my soul. It would kill me, and it had already started to kill one of the other boys. Camilo, a few years older than me, was called a viajero in the packs because he went wherever the women wanted to go. He would show them all around Oaxaca. The mountains, the beaches. He would go with them into other parts of Mexico, or other countries if they wanted. He'd come back with stories of hotels and parties, plane and boat rides, his clients being older and with money. He was twenty-one. The joke was that he probably had children all over the world.

"Camilo's life was the goal, Miguel Ángel said. He had done it himself, too, opening his services to any desire of his clients. I hadn't realized it yet that I too would do that in time, when the shy girl from Michigan came to town. But where Camilo, Miguel Ángel, and some of the other boys traveled away with anyone, I chose Joanne because she was different. Joanne had a mystery about her. She walked with her hands in her pockets, her eyes wide and innocent, aware that there was more to everything.

"One time, Camilo had returned from Guatemala after being with a girl for a few weeks, a red-haired backpacker from Los Angeles that wanted him to guide her into Central America. Camilo said he guided her all the way. This got them all going, laughing and asking for more. Half the time we never knew if Camilo was telling the truth. His tales of sex were so wild, maybe they were true. How could someone make up things like that?

"He took a few days off, then a few more. His group said he wasn't feeling well, that he had gotten sick even before he left to Guatemala. Maybe the trip made it worse. Maybe the food or the flu. Camilo came back to the zócalo for a few nights and only sat on the fountain steps. He began coughing so hard, he fell to the concrete. Enrique from his group noticed red spots on Camilo's arms, like bruises.

"Camilo never came back to the zócalo. He died later that year. It wasn't what some of the other boys had before, something they could fix with a cream or some pills. This was a new one. All the boys said how stupid Camilo was for not wearing condoms, and yet just weeks before he had returned, so many of them bragged that they only wore them if the woman wanted it, and did she ever really want one?

"I walked off that night, went home, and cried. What was it for? Why was I putting my myself through that? It had already been just over a year in the trade. The draft in my room, my stomach growling, my Papá moaning from his constant pain reminded me why: to stay alive. That's all life was—

surviving. The next night, Miguel Ángel brought me out and handed me a small bag from the pharmacy. It was filled with condoms. I shoved them back at him and said I quit. But he talked me back into it. He was a good salesman. He led me around the zócalo once again with his arm around my neck, like on the first night. 'It's summertime,' he said, 'The girls are arriving. Business is picking up.'"

5 - CHAPULINES

THE COLD AIR BLASTING INTO THE infirmary stops. Marcos licks his lips. He's thirsty. I am, too, but I don't want to call for anyone. I've always been like that. I try not to bother anyone. He wants more of the story. I have a cup of water in reach of my gurney, so I sit up, set the pages from Joanne aside and push the rolling tray over to him.

"Don't get up," Marcos says.

"Here, you're thirsty."

Marcos drinks. Looking at him makes me miss my family. My people.

"All of that on the zócalo—that was before you met Joanne?"

"Yes, I had been working the streets for two years when I met her. I was nineteen at the time."

"And Tío Miguel Ángel, he's the reason you stayed. Good thing, or you would not have met her, no?"

"Well, he was my instructor, at the very least. He taught me everything. He taught me bravery and swagger. He said you had to walk up to a tourist with complete confidence—attractive or not. You go to them, not them to you, he said. Most times, he said, they're not looking for anything, but how you approach them changes their mind. He had taught me about body language, facial expressions, tone of voice. Como ser un lobo con piel de cordero. Like a wolf in sheep's clothing. Learning to be confident helped me in general, but I was never as aggressive as Miguel Ángel. I always went for the ones that looked like they read the Bible. Not Miguel Ángel. He always went for the sinners, not the saints. Las aventureras. The girls who wanted only language lessons—someone to have coffee with—preserved my soul. I didn't feel dirty afterward, even when they paid. When they'd ask how much, I shook my head, shrugged. Miguel Ángel teased me for it.

"'What good is it to sit around and drink coffee with them trying to speak two different languages?' he said. 'You might as well go be a teacher. Get them in bed.'

"Later, I would thank him for the inspiration of my later profession.

"Joanne was one of them, one of the innocents. The night I met her, the lamps of the zócalo had flickered on in the early evening and covered in her long green dress and white shawl, her burlap woven bag slung in front of her, she looked warm, though she didn't need to be in the August air. A floppy hat covered half of her face and a camera covered the other half. She was framing a shot of the cathedral through the boughs of the trees. Miguel Ángel had spent more than enough time explaining women's clothing to me, and it often bothered me that he could only think in those terms. Had he seen Joanne, he would have said she was covered up too much and don't bother. She blended in but stood out at the same time, and how she slouched, making herself look smaller than she was. But yes, it was a signal she wasn't offering herself to anyone.

"I passed by her, slow and easy, my hands in my pockets. Miguel Ángel was always telling me to take my hands out of my pockets, said it made me look weak.

"'Take your picture?' I had asked her

"She glanced at me with a weak smile, clutching her camera. 'No, gracias.'

"Spanish. At least she tried. I moved ahead, didn't want to bother her. One head turn back, and I caught a glimpse of her face, its fine features, a lock of blonde hair tucked behind her ear, curling under her chin. She was young, like me. Her face stuck in my mind.

"On another lap of the zócalo, she passed me, and this time, she smiled, but not with her teeth. Just an acknowledgement. A gesture. I smiled back, nodded quick, not asking for anything.

"Behind me there was a voice.

36

"'Perdón,' she said.

"With such proper Spanish, I turned around.

"'Habla inglés?'

"'Sí. Yes.' I laughed, and it made her laugh.

"'Mercado Benito Juarez?'

"'Muy cerca. Very close.' I pointed. 'I walk you?'

"She said nothing, looking at me, studying me, evaluating me. They all did this, but not in this way. This was a measure of safety, not to check the merchandise.

"'Okay. Está bien.' This time she laughed.

"The walk to the mercado was silent. I stole a glance at her, just as she had stolen one of me. I had never seen a woman like her. It was as though her beauty was coming from inside of her—that her spirit was visible just under her skin.

"'Aquí estamos. Here we are.'

"'Gracias,' She looked ahead toward the mercado, now lit up with the lights over the busy booths and walkways, then back at me. She tilted her head just a bit, asking with her eyes, inviting me.

"'I join you? Me llamo Juan. Juan de Ortega.' I gave her my hand.

"'Joanne,' she said, shaking my hand.

"She was timid in the market, waving away offers from vendors to try a piece of this or that. She smiled and shook her head no at everything.

"'First time to Oaxaca?' I said.

"'Yes, first time out of the country. I'm nervous . . . Can you tell?'

"'Not to worry. I help you. Are you hungry?'

"'Yes.'

"'Let's start with tacos.'

"'That I know,' she smiled.

"We shared a plate of tacos al pastor and she drank from her bottle of Coke when the spice was too much.

"'Where are you from?'

"'U.S. I mean, Michigan. Muy lejos de aqui. El Norte.'

"'You're Spanish es muy bueno. Where you learn?'

"'Estoy estudiando en la escuela. En colegio. I mean, la Universidad. I want to live in a Spanish-speaking country one day.'

"'Mexico is the perfect place.'

"'My parents don't think so. They are scared for me. They worry too much.'

"She looked away, as though she was hiding something. She ate her last bite and pushed the plate.

"'I better go,' she said.

"'Back to Michigan?'

"She laughed. 'No, to my—where I'm staying.'

"'It's okay,' I said. 'I'm not going to hurt you.'

"She agreed to me walking her back to her hotel, though she wouldn't say the name. She only pointed *it's that way*.

"'¿Eres uno de las guías turísticas?' she said.

"'No soy uno de *estos*, los que te estás pensando.'

"You lied to her," Marcos interrupts. "You were one of *those* guides. But I think I know why. You didn't want to ruin it with her."

"You're right. It was as though I had finally found a friend, not a client. We said goodnight and agreed to meet the next day in the zócalo, same time, same place. We spent almost her whole visit together, the only time apart was when we said good night at the doorstep of her hotel every day. When I met her in the mornings, she had on her floppy hat and a backpack. It was clear she wanted just to talk and be with someone, and that was good with me. She lit up at everything and stopped to adore the smallest things: the worn cobblestones of the zócalo, the wail and thump of mariachi music, the grittiness of the champurrado. I loved this and I made me light up, too. Once, she took my hand and pulled me toward a woman walking a dog she wanted to pet. Joanne knelt down and asked the woman. The woman said yes, and Joanne pet the dog with one hand and squeezed my hand with her other. Joanne looked back at me, asking it seemed, if she could have a dog.

"The woman laughed and said, 'You need to get your girlfriend a puppy.'

"Joanne stood and kept hold of my hand.

"'She called me your novia,' Joanne said. 'I bet you have one already.

"Just then I did something I had never done with any other client. Miguel Ángel would have been furious, but he never knew.

"'I must tell you something,' I said, facing her, holding her hand. 'My name is Osvaldo Reyes. Not Juan De Ortega. You may call me Valdo.'

"'I knew that wasn't your real name,' she smiled and hit my arm. 'Come on. Let's go. Valdo.'

"She kept hold of my hand and we walked on to spend that morning like we always did: sitting at a café, drinking coffee, practicing her Spanish. We talked about being single or being taken and she laughed at the concept of prometido. Promised. She asked if I was prometido, and I said no, that I was un soltero. She blushed, and that was as much discussion we had about that subject. Looking back though, what we had felt was how it was supposed to be. There was no need to force anything. It was all happening by itself.

"When our conversations about home and family came up, she often changed the subject talking about her friends and her job more than anything. She worked at an ice cream shop that served food, a creamery, she called it. Oaxaca didn't have such places. She was proud of her job, and she said that was how she paid for her trips. She thought one day she might be a flight attendant, but that would make her parents—her father in particular, very unhappy.

"'My parents said if I want to travel, especially out of the country, then I have to pay for it myself. So that's what I'm doing. I have to see the world.'

"'Maybe bring your family for a visit?'

"She laughed, said that would never happen.

"'My parents believe they have everything they needed in the United States—why go anywhere else? My father was in the Korean War. He's a patriot and can't see anything else.'

"Back then, this made sense to me. I had never been outside of Mexico, and I didn't know anyone else who had, but what Joanne was saying, and I realize this now, is that her family was simply afraid. It was that fear she was trying to conquer for herself. Who knows, maybe she was trying to prove it to her parents, because it seemed like she wasn't making them proud by traveling across the border, especially the Mexican one.

"We had dinner together the last night—she paid for all of our meals—and afterward, I reminded her of what she had to do before leaving Oaxaca. I had said it the first night when we walked around the mercado. I had pointed out the wide woven saucers of chapulines that people either bought by the bag or the handful. I told her she had to try some, just a pinch. All week she avoided them until that last night.

"I asked for a taste and the vendedora waved Joanne to take some. Joanne took a small pinch out of the bowl and placed them in her palm. She studied them—lifted her hand to her nose and sniffed.

"'I can't believe I'm going to eat crickets,' she had said, and then she put them on her tongue and swallowed, appearing to choke them down. She smiled and stuck her tongue out to show she could do it. She gave me a small hit to my chest, her palm lingering over my heart.

"'See,' she said. 'I did it.'

"'And do you remember what that means?'

'That I'm destined to come back to Oaxaca, no?'

"'Sí, es correcto. Come on; I'll walk you back to your place.'

"That next day, her last in Oaxaca, we met for a coffee before she took the bus back to the airport. In the zócalo, the place we shared, she gave me a hug and brushed her lips against my stubbled chin—not quite a kiss—as she nuzzled into my neck. I held her, said to her with my body, *come back*.

"'I need your address," she had said, looking at her feet, not wanting me to see her eyes. "I will return to Oaxaca. I ate the chapulines, didn't I?'

"That was her first visit?" Marcos says.

"Yes, I think I felt love for her for the first time then. Something more than just friendship, and I think it felt that way because I knew I might never see her again. It was like I was holding onto something that would never be mine."

"But you kept in contact, no?"

"Yes, that started the letters. Joanne and I kept our friendship alive, and our language lessons, by sending each other letters. She always went on about how different she was from her friends and her family, that she was lonely in her own home. Her older sisters had married and had children, but Joanne had no interest. For a while, her family accused her of being lesbian. Her parents didn't understand her desires to travel to faraway places. When she told them she wanted to study Spanish, to major in it, her father almost cut her off. He made her choose education or nursing. She rebelled. She started going out to parties, staying out late. She tried alcohol and marijuana. It was like watching someone hurt themselves inside a locked cage. There was nothing I could do for her, only write to her and console her. I felt awful for what she was doing to herself, and yet, there I was, thousands of miles away, abusing myself, but in a different way.

For a while there, the letters stopped, and of course I thought something was wrong. I thought maybe her parents had found my letters. I thought maybe they had thrown her out for corresponding with a Mexican man. And then after a while, she wrote back, but it was a different voice. Someone troubled, and curious. She had asked me if I knew of Maria Sabina, the curandera, and whether I could take her to see her. Did you know of her?"

"No, but she sounds familiar," Marcos says.

"She was a shaman who lived in the Sierra Mazateca in Oaxaca in a village between the hills. She conducted rituals with mushrooms. Everyone in Oaxaca knew of her."

"She sold drugs?"

"No, it was medicine. She used the mushrooms to heal people, to help them see God."

"Had you visited her?"

"No, Maria Sabina was hard to find. And at that time, tourists—mostly hippie gringos—were flocking to Oaxaca to find her to have a healing, except their intentions were false. They simply wanted to have a trip and make fools of themselves. They abused the ritual. I was worried Joanne had become one of those hippies and only wanted to get high, but she began pleading to me in her letters saying she needed spiritual help. She was planning to visit later that summer and needed a healing."

"But for what?"

"She told me a part of her soul had died."

Marcos searches for an answer. Should I tell him? Are the secrets of others safe with strangers? Shouldn't I know now what can happen when you reveal too much of yourself to those who know nothing about you?

"She—she needed help, so I decided to help her. I told her Maria Sabina had stopped seeing foreigners, but that my madrina Adelina Ramos was a curandera, too, and had visited Maria Sabina more than once. Maria Sabina had healed Adelina, and Adelina had learned some of Maria Sabina's rituals. I told her that my madrina lived in the foothills of Puerto Escondido on the coast of Oaxaca. I said I would take her to see my madrina."

6 - LA VELADA

"ON HER SECOND VISIT, JOANNE ARRIVED in Oaxaca City on a Wednesday evening in early August and wanted to stay in the city for only one night, then spend the rest of her time, ten days, in Puerto Escondido. She had the whole plan. We took an overnight bus through the twisting sierras toward the coast, and Joanne had slept almost the entire way. She had nestled in close, tucked her petite body covered in a long blue paisley dress next to me, seeking warmth, it seemed, though the bus was warm. Undisturbed by the creaking of the bus at every turn in the road, she woke only once and asked for water. She sipped from my canteen, wiped her mouth, and went back to sleep. She was more tired this visit. Distant. Miguel Ángel said he knew exactly what women wanted by the smallest twitches in their eyebrows, or how their bottom eyelids lifted just a bit, tiny clues that showed if they were hungry, cranky, or in the mood. He was proud of me for taking one out of the city and teased me that I was finally going to have sex.

"But there on the bus, Joanne looked injured somehow. Those last couple of letters before she arrived, mixed in with her questions about meeting Adelina to have what was called a velada, she wrote more than a few times, 'Can I trust you?'

"Our bus arrived in Puerto Escondido at eight in the morning, and the jungle heat was overwhelming even at that hour. First, it was like a damp warm sheet draped over you, and if there were no clouds, which there usually weren't, the moisture dried just a bit, and then it began to bake. The end-to-end blue sky, so beautiful it almost hurt, did not mean calm forever. The rains—maybe even the hurricanes—were never that far away.

"In the shade of the whitewashed bus station she turned around for a hug, nearly tipping backward with her big traveling pack held up by her freckled shoulders. She had pulled her canvas bucket hat down over her sleepy eyes, tried to hide from the sun.

"'Are you hungry?' she said, yawning and looking back toward the Pacific far off on the horizon. 'I'm starving.'

"We wandered into Zicatela and found a quiet motel, Bungalows Las Brisas. On the patio, over a plate of chilaquiles and two jugos de naranja, the first Joanne—the happy and bright one—started to come back. Cocoa-brown surfer couples dusted in sea salt, tangled hair to their chins, wandered to their own tables, lit their morning cigarettes. Some smoked their marijuana right there as part of their breakfast.

"'You should grow your hair out,' she said. 'It'd look good on you.'

"'I have wild hair.'

"'That's why you should grow it.'

"'What you want to do today?'

"She looked at the plate, set her fork down.

"'I want to rest for a little while and write. Then maybe we can hike? Need to practice for the trip to the Sierra. To visit your godmother. Tu madrina.'

"'Está bien.'

"'And, Valdo, you don't have to serve me.' She rested her hand on mine. 'We're friends, remember?'

"Our room at Las Brisas had two beds, one closer to the door, and the other closer to the bathroom, so that they were spaced far apart. No air conditioning except a three-blade fan overhead. Joanne set her bag on the bed closest to the bathroom.

"'This one's mine,' she said.

"She closed the curtains, kicked off her sandals, and laid on the bed. 'Can you hold me?' she asked.

"Like her visit the summer before, there was no clear signal that she wanted to be naked—she only wanted to be close, bodies touching but not—

how two magnets push and pull against each other when one is reversed. There on the bed holding her, both of us clothed, I remembered the innocence of understanding a woman's body only through proximity. It was what made being with Joanne special—there were no carnal expectations. I too felt safe with her, unlike with the ones that only used my body.

"Sunday morning, before we left to go see Adelina, Joanne was in the bathroom getting ready. She was wrapped in a pink bath towel, her blonde hair smoothed down past her chin.

"'Hold me once more,' she said.

"I will never forget how we looked there in the in the chipped mirror, my arms encircling her body, two different skin tones, the steam still heavy in the small space.

"'We look like a couple,' she said. 'Like this is the future.'

"She often talked this way, as though she were remembering a dream, perhaps writing something in her head and needing to catch it before it got away. She wrote a lot that week, she said she was working on her book.

"I admit I kept trying to distract Joanne from going forward with the velada. The most I had ever done was smoke some marijuana and I didn't like it. I was nervous about doing anything like that with my Tía Adelina. I trusted Adelina—she was one of my mother's best friends, though I only saw her once or twice a year, sometimes not at all. I called Adelina before Joanne arrived in Oaxaca and asked her if we could visit. She was thrilled I was coming, I felt bad asking if she could conduct a healing.

"'Una velada,' she said. 'Ah, I should have known you only wanted to come here to get high.'

"She hung up, then called me back because she felt terrible, told me how much she missed me and wanted to see me.

"'And your friend,' she had asked. 'Your girlfriend?'

"I said yes to appease her. I couldn't tell her what I did for work, but she would get it out of me as I would later see.

"'You have to stay the night,' she said. 'You cannot come here and talk to God and just leave. Not like your uncles.'

"My Tía Adelina had never married, though she had been in a long relationship with my Tío Chano—she was his mistress. She was an outcast, which was sad because she was a kind and happy woman. Everyone thought she was a witch, a bad one. She had lived in Oaxaca City for many years then moved into the mountains to become closer to nature. That was when my family—except my Tío Chano of course—lost touch with her.

"Joanne and I hitchhiked out of Puerto Escondido then took a colectivo as far as the village of El Camarón along the Rio Colotepec. I always struggled to remember where Adelina exactly lived. In the hills, the tropical plants of the beaches gave way to the low-lying bushes surrounded by dry, dusty earth. I remembered the tienda in the town where Adelina shopped, collected her mail, and made her phone calls. She used to send me and my sister there to buy her cigarettes when we were young and when we stayed with her for a week or so in the summers.

"We crossed through her garden of maguey—Adelina also distilled her own mezcal—when a turkey strutted by. Joanne jumped and held onto me. It was her first visit away from the city and into the hills, and she seemed more vulnerable, more out of place than in Oaxaca City. I tapped on Adelina's screen door. Peeking in, it was dark like always.

"'Nina?' I called, but there was no answer. I pulled on the screen door and just as it opened Adelina appeared, small but strong, her hair still dark. She did what she always did: looked at me as though it was the first time she had seen me, pulled me into a hug I thought could break me, then made the sign of the cross with her thumb on my forehead—to prevent giving me mal de ojo, she said.

"She turned to Joanne shocked to see she was a gringa, yet she took her into a hug and held her. Joanne started to cry, and Adelina soothed her, shushed into her ear like she was calming a child.

"'You didn't tell me your girlfriend was American.'

"Joanne turned to me for translation. 'My tía says she's happy to meet you. And she calls you my girlfriend.'

"Joanne blushed. I took her hand as my godmother brought us inside. A dark hallway led to her living room where slivers of sunlight sliced through tiny gaps

46

in the closed curtains. In between pictures of Our Lady of Guadalupe and other saints covering the walls were candles and other religious artwork and carvings. The scents of herbs and oils, mixed with the odor of cigarettes and cooked onion and chiles filled her home like a cloud.

"'Come in,' she said and took my hand. 'I see it's time for your haircut.'

"One other thing Adelina always did when we reunited was cut my hair. She thought I was still a boy in this way. Adelina was my godmother, my barber, and my music teacher. She taught me how to play guitar. I've lost the skills—and I never really had them to begin with—though I learned early on that Adelina wanted to make the most of the times we had together, which is why she wanted to give me so much of herself.

"'No, Nina, it's fine, I don't need a haircut.'

"'Don't be silly,' she said. 'Come on.'

"There was no changing her mind.

"First, I bent my body to fit my head into her kitchen sink to wet my hair. She raked her fingers into my scalp lathering in a sweet shampoo. She rinsed my hair, dried it with a towel, and sat me down on a chair in the center of her kitchen. She gave Joanne a broom and motioned for her to sweep. She held me captive with scissors and asked me questions. It was there I told her things I never shared with anyone else, and where she educated me on things no one told me. She taught me about love and sex, life and death, how to live like you might not have another day, even if it meant hurting those you love. Adelina knew about my first romances, my family's troubles, and in little bits she pulled out me what I did on the zócalo, our exchanges too quick for Joanne to understand.

"Adelina didn't chastise me. She crossed my forehead again and whispered to me that I was smart and knew how to take care of myself. She turned her attention to Joanne and began speaking broken English, to which Joanne replied with her elementary Spanish. Sweeping up my hair, Joanne shared her own troubles: her father, who, though Joanne hadn't admitted it to me, was a racist, and how Joanne wanted to be far away from her family. She spoke about the other students at her school—the boys—and how cruel they were. Translating this to Adelina, I knew Joanne was still hurt inside by something, and Adelina didn't pry. The two of them seemed to share an intuition, and Adelina, as she clipped my hair, told me to tell Joanne that she would help her find the light again.

"Adelina dusted the hair off of my neck and face and told me to take my shirt off.

"'While your shirt is off,' she said, 'Go kill the turkey.' She opened a drawer and handed me a long knife.

"This was also a test, to see if the city had turned me into a coward, and, I believed, to show Joanne that I had the strength to do it.

"'What does she want?' Joanne asked.

"'For me to kill the turkey.'

"'But I thought . . .'

"'No, it's not her pet,' I said. 'It's our dinner.'

"By that afternoon, the hot weather cooled, but the spit in Adelina's yard with the turkey roasting and her stove top bubbling with the sweet and smoky scents of the mole coloradito she was cooking, kept her kitchen warm. We sat for an early dinner before the sun had set, and afterward, Adelina instructed us to rest and pray. She offered a pipe with marijuana to smoke. Joanne puffed on it and then closed her eyes. I smoked some, then gave it back to Adelina.

"'You rest now,' Adelina said.

"I closed my eyes and feel asleep for what felt like hours. When I woke, I was covered in a blanket and the candles in her living room were all lit. Joanne was still asleep, too.

"'I think we're too tired,' I said to Adelina who had come back into the room with three cups.

"'No,' she said. 'You needed the rest, and your food needs to digest.'

"She came over to me and rubbed my shoulders. 'Don't worry,' she said, 'Everything will be fine. You are safe with me. Drink this, then wake her up.'

"'What time is it?'

"'It's time,' she said.

"I woke Joanne, and she took a deep breath and stretched. She smiled at me and stood up, her face ready with resolve.

"'Where's Adelina?' she said.

"'She said to wait here. She said she was getting the children.'

"'Ah, yes. That's what Maria Sabina calls them. I read it in an article.'

"Adelina entered just as Joanne said that, answering her, 'Sí, los niños—the children.' She set a tray down with a small clay pot, three glasses and a bottle of clear liquid. She motioned for us to sit. Saying nothing, she knelt next to the table and uncorked the bottle and the distinct smokiness of mezcal wafted from the glass. She poured a small amount in each glass then dipped her thumb in one, then made the sign of the cross on Joanne first, then repeated it with the next glass and my forehead until she finished by crossing herself.

"She stood and brought over three candles that were up on her alter, each white and in tall glass jars. She set them on the table and brought praying hands to her mouth. Her lips moved slow and calm and still in silence. She motioned for us to kneel with her. As our knees touched the floor, she lit the three candles and we followed her lead, our hands to our lips, eyes closed. It felt like we prayed for longer than we slept, and I don't remember at all what I asked for, if I asked for anything at all. What broke the silence was Adelina placing her hand on my chest. Eyes open, she had a hand on me and a hand on Joanne. Adelina moved her hands off of us, then turned to the small tray and small bowl. Inside rested three mushrooms with long dry and shriveled stalks and a tiny bulb at the top that had the faintest streaks of purple and yellow.

"Adelina herself took one of the mushrooms and placed it on her tongue. She closed her mouth and began moving her jaw up and down though she was not chewing. At last she swallowed, then closed her eyes and kept them closed. Joanne looked at me trembling, waiting for instruction. I shrugged and shook my head. I had never done it either, and I felt at that moment we should not have been doing that. I thought of Joanne's family—her father, whom I had never met—what would I do if something terrible happened, if Joanne went crazy or died. What would I do then?

"Adelina opened her eyes and offered the bowl to Joanne and me. She dipped her chin with a peaceful expression.

"'The journey will start later. You may feel ill. That's when you know it has begun.'

"Joanne and I took our pieces and we placed them in our mouths. Adelina reached forward and laid her hands on us, mumbling with eyes closed again. The taste was bitter, like dirt, and though it was tough to chew, like a soft twig or blade of grass, it disintegrated quickly. I remember lying back into the couch where we first sat, then later onto the floor where Adelina had laid out blankets and pillows. She had begun chanting, her voice even and calm, the words sounded like prayer, but they began to fade into a hum, and then I felt nauseous. Adelina had a bowl to catch the vomit and she cleaned my mouth. Joanne was next. Adelina soothed our foreheads with a cool wet cloth and tucked us into the blankets.

"Soon after, I began to travel to places I had never been before. I was both on earth and in heaven. I was inside my body and out. When I kept my eyes closed, I saw deep into a universe filled with colors and patterns, and when I had my eyes open, everything swayed and melted into one thing. Sounds and sights were all one sensation. I remember digging my fingers into the blanket I was lying on and feeling every single fiber, and not just feeling it, but feeling connected to it. I know, it's strange to describe."

"And Joanne, how was she?" Marcos asks.

"She started out quiet. She lay in the blanket on her side as if she was going to go back to sleep. She flung her arm out grabbing and Adelina went to her with the bowl. After Joanne vomited a second time, she chanted along with Adelina. Joanne was making the sounds of the words and it's possible she understood them too. Adelina stayed calm through all of the journey and kept close to Joanne. After her chanting, Joanne started to laugh, and it was a laugh I had never heard. That was when I—even though I was somewhere else myself—began to worry about her. She said nothing but just laughed with her whole body until her face dampened with tears. I reached for her once and Adelina stopped me, held my hand, petting my forearm to calm me.

"Joanne's laughter changed to tears, and she rolled up into a ball.

Adelina continued to soothe her, shushing her like a baby, patting her back. Adelina began to pray over Joanne until she relaxed, and then Joanne began speaking about the colors. 'Oh, the colors,' she said. 'The colors are so beautiful.'

"Later, and this part is a blur, Joanne got up from our blankets on the floor and walked around the room. She went to the candles and warmed her hands over some of them and knelt and prayed in front of others. Adelina gave her some juice and my last vision was of Joanne sitting again on the couch smiling holding her juice with a glow surrounding her entire head and shoulders. She looked like a little girl happy with her juice, her innocence restored.

"I don't know what happened next because I fell asleep and had dreams I won't ever have again. I am certain at one point I left my body and floated over the ocean and was then summoned back to my skin with the rooster's call just at daybreak. I believe my soul had slipped back into my flesh and as my eyes fluttered open, I was still where I was on Adelina's floor, nestled in a blanket. From the corner of my eyes, I saw Joanne's toes sticking out from a blanket. She must have fallen asleep on the couch and Adelina covered her. I didn't spring up. I wanted to stay in that cocoon. The journey reminded me to stay protected, to keep my body safe. In those waking moments I thought of Miguel Ángel and the other boys of the zócalo. What were we doing to ourselves? How could we let that happen to us as though it was nothing?

"As the rooster kept crowing, I began to wiggle my feet and hands and tense my muscles. I was all there—I had returned unharmed. Adelina was correct: I was safe with her. As I sat up, my godmother came over to me and kissed me on top of the head. She had a steaming cup of coffee, and I have never smelled anything so delicious in my life. I looked over at Joanne who was still tucked away sleeping. Adelina put her finger to her lips and shushed.

"'The girl has found the light again,' she said."

MARCOS SHAKES HIS HEAD in disbelief. "This is unbelievable, tío. You took a mushroom trip? I thought those were only legends. What our ancestors did."

All I can offer Marcos is a shrug of my shoulders. My voice has become tired from all the talking and my body says it might be time to eat. You never can tell when there are no windows. The mail arrived this morning, I know that much, and Nurse Vargas has not returned for a while. Maybe she will be back soon. Marcos still looks uncomfortable. They've given us pills for our pain. If only they had something to remove uncertainty—to take away the fear of not knowing what will happen next. I drink some water. It satisfies me, reminds me I'm a human and not an animal. Marcos begins to drift off. He needs to rest, and so do I.

7 - MOTEL CALIFORNIA

MY EYES POP OPEN AND I REALIZE I'm still in the infirmary. Marcos is in his bed, sleeping. I don't know how long I was asleep, but I know I wasn't there for a period of time during my nap. I had left myself. It happened again. It was short though, just a quick step away from my body. That talk of the velada must have triggered it. The velada wasn't the first time I had left myself.

The first was when I was bitten by a snake as a young boy. My father and uncle brought us kids to see the ruins of Monte Albán to remind us of our indigenous heritage. It was summer and blinding hot. On the carretera, my uncle's truck ran out of gas. The men yelled at another truck to stop. They went to town and me and my cousins waited and waited. Two fell asleep in the bed of the truck, but me and another went looking around. Kicking at rocks far from the side of the road, I saw a bush with something shiny. I went to it, pushed my foot into it thinking it was a rock, but it moved—the jerk was faster than anything I had and will ever see in my life— telling me that it was alive and much stronger than me. The needle stings of the serpent penetrated my ankle through my denim, and I kicked back, knocking it away from me. I fell to the dirt, dust clouds encircling me, crawling backward and screaming as though I was dying.

My last memory was the taste of that dust, then the feeling of my body breaking into hundreds of tiny pieces. I came back together and felt as though I was flying, looking down on myself, my cousin over me calling out for help, then running back toward the road.

I continued to float upward, nothing around me but blue sky, then a force yanked at me, like a huge hand, pulling me. I tried to fight it, but it was too strong. I let it take me as the blue sky turned into the brightest light I'd ever seen. My ears flooded with the sound of a thousand people whispering, calling to me. Later, I woke in a clinic somewhere near Monte Albán. My dad and my uncle and cousins stood around me crying and laughing.

The only people I ever told about that journey was Adelina, and later Joanne, and finally Teresa. Adelina I told close to when it happened. She said being that close to God was a gift and that I should honor it. She said it had probably awakened a power in me that could be used for good. I was too young to make sense of what she said, but her words came back to me the morning after our velada. I remembered there was an entire universe inside of me—inside of my head—that could be explored.

After the velada, Joanne and I said goodbye to Adelina, hitchhiked back down into Puerto Escondido, then caught our return bus back to Oaxaca. Joanne had kept quiet that morning after. She drank the coffee and ate some fruit Adelina gave us, but Joanne went to writing in her journal. She did that all morning and seemed to be deep in thought, though she looked calm and relaxed. On the bus ride back, she at last opened up, said she had been bathed in a comforting and colorful warmth in which a voice spoke to her, said to always follow the light. That was after she had fallen into a darkness of terrible and dangerous thoughts accompanied by the feeling that her soul was slipping away. That was when I shared that I had left myself during the velada, and also as a child after the snake bite. Joanne thought it was scary but amazing.

Years later, well into married life and fatherhood, I began to have a recurring dream. In it I wander the zócalo at night. No one is around, and everything is closed. I try to open a door to a shop where I see a faint light. Once inside, I go to it, walking in pitch darkness toward the flicker. I get closer, reaching for it, but it keeps moving away from me. I begin running to it, grabbing at it, and when I believe I have a hold on it, the light becomes a small reptilian eye, and the darkness, daylight. Then, I'm standing in the desert, my bare foot stepping on a snake. It bites me and begins to swallow up to my ankle. Sometimes it goes as far up as my calf or knee. I scream and try to shake it off, but it will not let go. I've never let the snake eat past my thigh, always waking myself before it bites my hip.

In those times of the recurring dream, I told my wife Teresa. She wasn't one to believe in the supernatural, but when it came to dreams, Teresa had read books and studied them. She had kept journals. She had known about the snake bite, so she reminded me that dreams like that—the ones that haunt were just that: ghosts.

"Your child brain is still recovering from that traumatic experience," she had said. "The snake bite itself will always be imprinted in your mind."

She made it all sound so normal, like a diagnosis. Then I told her about my near death. She acknowledged it, said it was interesting, but then shrugged her shoulders.

"Who knows what happens after we die,' she said. "Let's only hope it's beautiful."

MARCOS WAKES UP. "I'm hungry," he says.

"Me, too. I don't know when she's coming back."

"That story, man, I never would have thought. You, a wild man in another life."

"It was another life. And you. You have ghosts, too, I imagine."

"No, I'm boring. Nothing like yours. My wife—she was my first. I'm a good boy."

"The world needs more men like you and less like me."

"Stop that, tío. You've had a good life."

He's right. My life has been blessed. I am lucky. My problem is I keep making bad decisions.

"So," Marcos says. "Afterward, what? She was cured? I still don't know why she was in trouble."

"Because you are a good man, I will tell you. Joanne had kept it a secret until our last meeting, when we met in Ensenada in Baja California, not too far from here. She had come to San Diego for an interview at the University and had only two nights to visit. The plan was to meet near Ensenada, north Baja—our third visit in three years, each one a step further along a path never taken with any other client. But remember, I never thought of Joanne as a client.

"I only had money for bus fare and so I went from Oaxaca City to Puebla and rode all the way to Sonora, then on through Mexicali and eventually to Rosarito. It took more than a day it seemed. She had found a place on the coast highway north of Ensenada called Motel California. The red tile roof adobe sat as close as it could on a bluff overlooking the Pacific. The room had a view of the ocean and one bed.

"Once in the room, it felt like it always did, whether it was with an experienced client or Joanne—those awkward settling-in moments of putting bags down and deciding over beds never was quite right. Joanne unzipped one of her smaller bags and pulled out a stack of paper bound by three gold fasteners. The clean front page said—*Slip Soul*—By Joe DeVries.

"'Your book?' The fresh printed ink looked puffy on the page, not as it does today.

"'Yes. After the velada with Adelina, the whole thing just spilled out of me. I wrote everything down. I wanted to share it with you.

"'Joe DeVries? You?'

"'It's a pen name.' She shrugged, hid her eyes.

"'Why?'

"'DeVries is my mother's maiden name.' Joanne had begun slowly pacing around the room. 'I don't know. I thought if I wrote it—as a man—I guess it might be . . . it's hard to explain. I don't want people to know it's me. And it's not very kind to the American.'

"'The Mexicano—he travels in his sleep, no?'

"'I'm still working on it. I don't like the ending.' She lifted her chin, blinked. 'Will you read it?'

"'Yes, I will,' I said.

"She stood and walked over to the sea-facing window and pulled open the curtains. June along the California coast stayed gloomy until midday and sometimes never cleared. Now and then the clouds would part, and the sun—just before it fell into its watery bed for the night—would peek out and flash green.

"'Remember my second visit? When we went to Zicatela, how I only wanted you to hold me?' She sat next to me on the bed. I thought then if we had never made love, it would be fine—I loved her that much. The rest of them only used me. Once in a great while they gave me something besides money. A necklace. A new shirt. Some shoes.

"'Sí, claro.'

"She'd matured a bit more since that trip. Streaks of brown were starting to come in under her blonde hair—it was shorter now—and her hips and thighs had rounded since her backpacking days. She was more womanly than I had remembered.

"'I wanted to tell you something, but I couldn't. I hurt so much back then,' she said.

"'What happened, Juana? You can tell me. Soy tu amigo.'

"'Before I saw you that second time, before I came to Mexico for the summer, something bad happened to me back home in Michigan.'

"She began to tremble and put her hand on her stomach. I thought she might be ill.

"'There was a boy at school.' Joanne lowered her eyelids and reached for my hand. 'I can't even say his name.'

"'What happened? What did he do?' I held her shoulders.

"'He killed something in me. I needed to heal.'

"How I used to kill myself with my own body. The profession, if it could be called that, meant giving that same part of myself away every time. Most times I gave, other times, they wanted me to take. Once, a girl had cried afterward, but she assured me it was fine, that there was nothing I did to hurt her. Others lit a cigarette, some wanted me to hold them. Many simply left or fell asleep, money on the table. Sometimes they gave a kiss on the cheek and said thank you. Either way, it was an agreement between two people—a transaction. What happened to Joanne, the way she still held herself together, was a violation.

"'It was why you wanted to take the hongos, no?'

"'Yes, to become new. I thought she could help me. I thought you could help me, too.'

"'Yo?'

"'There's something special about you, Valdo.'

"My Tío Miguel Ángel had never married, never had kids. He spent his whole life on the parranda because he knew nothing else. He was hooked. You can be a zócalo boy for as long as you like, just as long as you got what it takes, he always said, and that's why he was so good at it. But some of the boys didn't do it forever. They grew up to become men. They made their money. Paid for their education. Started a new life with someone they loved. She was the reason to quit the zócalo. There was something special about her.

"'Juana, I miss you. I think about you. I want to protect you. I want to be with you.'

"'I do too,' she said, squeezing me, planting her lips on my neck, her kisses damp from her tears. With my mouth on her collar bone, I kissed her softly. Never had it gone this far, but I held myself back, knowing she had been destroyed by someone else—a man—and may not want any touch. And yet, she embraced me, her fingers pressing into my skin, her lips not leaving my body, like nothing I had received from anyone else.

"Between breaths, she said, 'I wish you had been my first.' She took my hand and placed it over her chest, then guided my fingers in between the spaces of the buttons on her blouse.

"The curtain stayed open all night, bare skin to bare skin never coming apart. From the light of the moon shining on the sea, I captured her small face with its fine features, the face I pictured when she talked about the girl named Alice who stood at the edge of a large mushroom talking to the hookah-smoking caterpillar. Joanne had shared that story on the hike into the Sierra Mazateca to see Adelina. Joanne had talked about Wonderland, and how in the end, Alice figured out it was all just nonsense."

Marcos can only shake his head. I know I am shocking him at every turn. I debate if I should tell him more.

"The velada helped her," he says, "but you helped her, too. With your love. And I don't mean the sex."

"That's it. I never wanted anything more. Our friendship was the most important to me, and I suspected she was in pain, even before she told me about her rape. That weekend in Ensenada—it's hard to explain—but it was both beautiful and painful. I think we both knew somewhere inside ourselves we wanted that—to know each other's bodies—yet it was forbidden in its own way."

"Maybe that's what she meant by you having something special. You protected her."

"I think you're right. I think that's why we were put together in the first place. And that's why we tried to keep our relationship going. That's what all those letters were for after Ensenada."

"And the book, no?" Marcos says. "That's her real love letter to you. You're going to read it to me, aren't you?"

"I don't know. It will take time."

Marcos looks around. "Are you going somewhere? Come on, tío. Read some to me."

"It's in English."

"I know the country I was coming to, tío. Read it."

"Fine. A couple of chapters."

The pages look almost the same, still held together by three gold fasteners. The front page has ripped off. I smooth it over, turn to the first page, and start reading to Marcos.

Slip Soul by Joe DeVries
Chapter 1

Zicatela, Oaxaca, Mexico, 1978

Fridays were the busiest day at Los Bungalows de Las Brisas. It was the day many guests checked out, taking their stories and worries, and their hangovers and dreams with them. Pablo Garza, owner of the seaside motel, imagined that they took a little part of his town with them every time they left, and he hoped they would return it when they came back. He loved repeat visitors who returned like family to their long-lost home.

Friday was also when the most guests checked in. New people arrived wide-eyed and weary carrying their hopes and heartaches in big backpacks on their shoulders and clutching little empty journals in their hands. Most arrived by bus from Oaxaca City; an overnight trip on the two-lane Devil's Backbone twisting through the Sierra, while others came by car with their maps in shreds upon their arrival, and some souls simply washed up on the seashore.

That August afternoon, three new arrivals to the Bungalows caught Pablo's attention in a way no other travelers had. They arrived as a trio, and it was unclear at first who might have been with whom, or if there was an underlying relationship amongst them, except for the two women, who Pablo believed were related.

It wasn't uncommon for a man to arrive with two women. There were all kinds of pairs and combinations that checked in. There were the couples, the groups of friends, the families, and of course, the solo travelers. Of these pairings, they were usually alike in some way. These three were each quite different.

The man of the trio was large and athletic, not like the lean surfers that flocked to Playa Zicatela, and, he was a gringo, most certainly from the United States donning a military haircut. But he was familiar in some way, as through Pablo knew him from somewhere. With him were two beautiful women with black skin and thick wavy hair. One was thin and petite, her hair pulled into a tail with the length of it resting on her shoulder, and the other was built sturdy with robust features, her hair held back with a head band.

Most of Pablo's guests were Mexican, followed by Americans, and then Central and South Americans, so it was unusual to see two of African descent, and of their beauty he was transfixed, particularly toward the smaller one. All three of the people had a story. Pablo had developed an ability to read such stories on the faces of guests the moment they checked in—yet hers was difficult to decipher. He sensed a certain loneliness in her, a mild sadness, while at the same time he had an instant attraction toward her.

The big man was the dominant of the three as he stepped forward to the front desk. He began with decent Spanish:

"One room, two beds, please."

Pablo responded: "How long will you be staying? And do you prefer to be on the first or second floor?"

The man seemed lost to which Pablo switched to English, but the bigger girl spoke up, her Spanish perfect and with a hint of French in her accent.

"Two rooms, if you have them, one for me, and one for them, but it depends on the price. And we'll be staying ... a week, maybe more."

"We have the rooms. 800 for double, 900 for single."

"One room." the man stepped forward, setting his hand on the counter.

"Very well." Pablo pushed the leather-bound register toward them with a smile, trying not to look at the young lady. "Please sign in here. Please pay the first night, and we—I—will provide a final bill at checkout."

The man scribbled their names in fast as though he wanted to get on with it.

Lester Brooks.

Jucélia Duran.

Renata Duran.

Pablo turned to get a key hanging up in the box with hooks behind him. He turned to find the money on the counter.

"Where are you from?" he asked, studying the man's face. It occurred to Pablo, who also had a great memory for faces, that this man was someone known. A celebrity. No, he thought. An athlete. *A luchador?* A big fan himself, Pablo knew there were the occasional foreigners in the sport, and they were often the *rudos*.

"The United States," the big man said, taking the petite girl by her waist into his arm. "My girlfriend here, Jucélia, and her sister are from Brazil."

"Renata," the other girl said, extending her hand to Pablo. She had a delicate grip, yet she held Pablo's hand longer than expected.

Jucélia smiled, her eyes lingering on Pablo for a moment, then she looked away. Pablo noticed this and returned her glance, his curiosity for her now piqued.

"Is there a good restaurant around?" the man said. "We're starving."

"Yes, Los Tíos, just down the malecón here," Pablo turned his attention back to the man, and that's when he made the connection. "I'm sorry," Pablo continued, "but I think I know you. Are you—were you ... a luchador? A wrestler."

The man chuffed up his chest, a smile spread across his face. Renata rolled her eyes.

"Yes, yes I am," he said.

"Rugger?" Pablo said. "El Rugerio de Australia?"

In the pantheon of luchadores, there was el Rugerio de Australia, a supposed Australian man from the outback of the distant continent that could subdue a crocodile with his bare hands. He wore Australia's green and gold on his mask and wore green pants. He fought in the circuit against the great técnicos of Mexico, then fell from popularity after he was unmasked.

"That's me," Lester said. "Ruggy. You can call me Ruggy. Everyone still calls me Ruggy, right, girls?"

He still held Jucélia close to him with Renata standing by, impatient with it all.

"Well, I'm a big fan ..." Pablo said, and Ruggy beamed, "of la lucha. Every time I'm in Oaxaca City I go to the ring. The best are in Mexico City."

"That's where I—" Ruggy went on, but Pablo cut into his sentence.

"Come, I'll take you to your room and show you around Los Bungalows de Las Brisas."

Ruggy frowned at this, but Pablo had turned his attention to the women and didn't notice as he led them out of the lobby.

"Here is the patio." Pablo stopped to show them a large common space at the center of the motel that was surrounded by a short white stucco wall and topped by a dried palm palapa roof with a few gaps in the weaves, through which sunlight poured onto the flagstone floor. A couple of hammocks hung between two of the support beams, and lounge chairs and small tables filled in the rest of the space. Toward the ocean-facing wall stood a workstation with a grill and preparation counter covered in blue tile.

"We have breakfast here in the mornings," Pablo said. "Café, jugo, panes. I'll make some eggs if you ask." He smiled at them—Jucélia and his eyes meeting and locking on each other for a moment. He turned away, knowing she was with Lester. "And tonight, hora feliz at 6 pm. Beer, tequila, rum."

He led them toward a modest garden bordered by bougainvillea and small cactus and two tiled walkways where the rooms began. He was taking them to the largest room in the motel. It was the room behind his apartment, which was, at one time, part of the residence he shared with his parents when they were alive. Along with two beds spaced far apart, the room had a small side space with a sofa. Maybe the sister, Renata, could use that as her area to have a sense of privacy.

"The owners have done a nice job," Ruggy said.

"It's not those grand hotels near the Bahía but thank you."

"You're the owner?" Ruggy said. "You're so young."

Pablo smiled. "My family business. My parents started when I was very young."

"They must be very proud," Renata said. Pablo cast his eyes down and nodded. Too soon to say that his parents were no longer among the living.

"And tonight, if you're interested, there's a bar just north on the malecón, it's the closest one to here, called La Sirena. Cold beer and some food. Good music."

"We'll come by," Ruggy said.

"Did you drive here?" Pablo stopped them in front of the room, handed the key with the plastic diamond-shaped ornament.

"Yes, from Mexico City. It's been a long drive," Ruggy said. "I was telling you that I was there for la lucha."

"Well, you must be tired. And what part of Brazil are you two from—" He paused, smiling at the women.

"São Paolo," Jucélia said. Just then Ruggy took her again by her waist.

"I have always wanted to visit Brazil," Pablo said. "Settle in and put your things down and tell me if you need anything."

He turned to leave the trio and go back to the lobby so he could prepare the tubs of beer for hora feliz and practice his guitar for later that night at La Sirena. By night, Pablo sang at the bar on a small stage in the corner with his cousin Jorge, who added percussion and the occasional trumpet. Pablo glanced over his shoulder as his new guests were turning the key in the lock, and there again, his eyes met with Jucélia's as though the two of them were waiting for that specific moment of privacy. She smiled, at last free from Ruggy's grip, then went into the room.

Late that night, after La Sirena closed, Pablo and Jorge left the bar with their instruments followed by the new visitors. They had closed the place after Pablo was done with his set, and after they'd had a few shots of tequila.

"You didn't tell us you were the star," Ruggy swatted Pablo's arm.

"You were wonderful," Renata said.

"Great time," Jucélia said. "Thank you."

"Let's go end the night on the beach," Jorge said.

"They're tired," Pablo said. "Been traveling all day."

"We're fine," Renata said, and pulled her sister away from Ruggy. He held onto her hand pulling Jucélia back toward him.

Out on the beach in front of the Bungalows, Jorge had brought leftover beer from hora feliz and began rolling a cigarette. Pablo opened his case and strummed again on his guitar. Above them, a crescent moon hung just over the shimmering ocean, the waves still as powerful as during the day.

Jorge lit his creation and puffed. "You smoke?"

"Is that what I think it is?" Renata smiled and took the joint. It came around to Ruggy, but he passed and shot Jucélia a look not to. Pablo took a quick puff and continued to play quiet melodic chords.

"You live in paradise," Ruggy said.

"It's nice," Pablo said. "It's hurricane season though." He stopped strumming.

"You'd never know," Jucélia said.

Pablo looked at her and under the moonlight glow he felt the electricity of something new inside of him. It was similar to the sensation he felt when he drifted off to sleep at night, just in the space between asleep and awake, when the body is relaxing, and the mind is still racing, the spirit plotting its course for the night.

The group stayed only for a while, and as they started back toward the Bungalows, the pairings were evident. Jucélia and Ruggy, and Renata and Jorge—the two had been giggling and flirting after the bar. Pablo wished them goodnight and went back to his place behind the lobby. In the darkness he got into bed, alone again, and anticipated what was coming.

Some nights he could control his body's release of his soul, and the journeys outside of his flesh that followed. Other nights, he had no control, and others, he simply had dreamless sleep. Either way, he reminded himself that he was not dying, that he would not die on one of these trips, and that he should, as his madrina Tía Claudia always said, "Embrace your gift."

"Ah, I see," Marcos says. "You are Pablo. And Joanne is Jucélia."

"That's how I see it too."

"She turned herself into a black Brazilian woman," Marcos says. "Amazing."

"She's the writer. She has an imagination."

"And she wanted to be someone else," Marcos says. "She wanted to escape the man. The luchador. That was her rapist, no?"

"You're right."

"Keep reading," Marcos says. "I want to hear more."

Slip Soul by Joe DeVries
Chapter 2

That night was one of those dreamless sleeps, and Pablo felt better for it the next morning. On the nights he traveled, there was a residual physical feeling, he thought, due to the sensations that accompanied the separation, as though he was still buzzing with energy.

That's how they commenced: while lying down and already in a light sleep, the feeling of low-level electricity began in one extremity or another. A foot.

A hand. Both feet, both hands. Then the sensation increased, as though someone was turning up a dial, the feeling spreading to the larger parts of his body—his chest, hips, shoulders, head. And then there was the separation itself, when his spirit lifted from his body and began to drift. This too was different every time. Sometimes he lifted upward, other times he sunk under his body. Once, it seemed as though he was being pulled by his feet, like someone opening a drawer.

The first experience outside of his body, and what Pablo believed was the beginning of it all, was when he was young and nearly died in the surf. When they were about eleven years old, he and Jorge had paddled out alone on their surfboards into the morning waves of the Bahía Principál before all the *lancheros* could ruin the water with their little motorboats filled with fat *turistas* hoping to see a *tortuga*.

The breaks were smaller and easy that day. They had ridden a few of Playa Zicatela's *olas* in the low season, with Jorge's dad, Luis, on *tablas* next to them. When in doubt, go under, he told the boys.

But no need to go under that morning. The boys had spent most of the time sitting up on their boards, gazing into the endless horizon, the sun glistening off their browned backs and black hair.

They knew not to turn their backs on the ocean, to always face the waves. But boys test limits. They push on things, waiting for them to snap. Once past the break on the glassy sea, Pablo stood on his board, balanced like a small Jesus walking on water. Jorge laughed, splashed his cousin. Pablo tiptoed up and down the board. No waves in sight. He turned toward the beach. Puerto Escondido, *tranquilo*. The village still sleeping off the hangover, like Pablo's father.

Tío Luis taught them about the sets. A series of big ones are usually seven minutes apart, and in between that time, the ocean may feel calm, but be careful. Sometimes the creepers come up and grab you.

Pablo was toward the front of his six-foot board when one of them appeared. It was too sudden for Jorge to warn his cousin. It curled fast, almost silent. Pablo scrambled to center himself, but he tumbled headlong; face to water, his body twisting in *la lavadora salada*—the salty washing machine, they called it. A bad spin in the rinse cycle could pound you straight down onto the sea floor.

He remembered the thump of his head knocking the firm sand below, then a short blackout, followed by the departure. It happened quick and with no sensations. He had snapped out of his flesh, and his soul went up into the air, high enough to see his capsized body float to the surface, then rush into the churning waves. His ghost body fell back into his flesh the moment his real body rolled up the soft sand, where the water calmed to a band of white bubbles. He sat up, as though waking from a terrible amazing dream, and laughed.

Jorge paddled up. "What happened?"

Wild eyed, Pablo couldn't contain himself.

"I died and came back!" he said. "I flew up into the sky!"

He was hysterical the rest of the morning.

"Enough for you today," Jorge helped him up. "You didn't die, *tonto*. Get up."

"But I went somewhere." Pablo pointed up.

"Forget it. Come on, let's go."

In his conversations with his Tía Claudia, she called his ability a hidden doorway—*una puerta escondida*—and that once it was opened, he might go through it again and again. This morning, as he came to wakefulness, the door remained shut, though his mind wandered remembering what today was—the anniversary. He couldn't believe it was time. Tía Claudia would be on her way later that day.

Wiggling his toes to wake up, he shifted his thoughts to his new guests just on the other side of the wall. Were they comfortable? Was it enough space? He thought about the women, and did the taller one, Renata, go home with Jorge? And Jucélia, how she kept making eye contact. He dwelled on her for a moment, and thought of what might be, how he, now single once again, could be more for her than him. It was clear there were problems in that relationship.

Pablo got out of bed and dressed and went to work setting out the morning's food for the guests, brewing the coffee, arranging the pastries and fruit. He turned on the record player that spun with Bob Marley. Pablo loved this part of the day, when the world was his and his only.

Jorge was probably not going to show. He was good help when he was there, but only when he was there. Pablo did have Perla and Cristina who cleaned rooms and helped on busy weekends, and Gustavo the old gardener who came every other Friday. Sometimes a kind guest already up and swinging in a hammock would offer to help set up, but most of the time it was just Pablo.

Wiping tables Pablo hadn't noticed someone standing on the other side of the one of the support beams of the palapa. Just where the cobblestone street met the sand, Ruggy faced the ocean, arms crossed, surveying the clear horizon. Pablo approached him, still fascinated that a real luchador had checked into Los Bungalows de Las Brisas.

"Señor Rugerio?" Pablo hoped not to pull him from his deep thinking.

Ruggy turned to Pablo's voice, his chest uncovered and sweating in the already hot sun.

"Morning," he said.

"You're awake early," Pablo said.

"I went for my morning run," Ruggy said, holding his shirt in his hand. Pablo realized how much the man loomed over him, how much space he took, even in the openness of the beach.

"How is the room?" Pablo asked.

"It's nice. Quiet. The girls are still asleep. You have a nice place here."

"I am very lucky," Pablo looked out to the horizon. "Do you want coffee?"

"No, not for me." Ruggy began walking back along the low stucco wall to come back into the property. He put his shirt back on and seemed more normal, less of the performer he was in the lucha ring. "I wanted to ask, are you playing tonight at the bar—what was it called? La—"

"La Sirena? No, not tonight. I have . . . something else to do."

"You're very good," Ruggy said. "You should be playing in all the bars on this beach."

"Well, thank you," Pablo said. "Only something I do once in a while. Are you back to fighting?"

Ruggy, now under the palapa with Pablo, looked away.

"Taking a break. Injuries. That's why we are here. To rest."

"Take all the time you need. You three came at a good time—the end of summer. After this, it's quiet."

"What about you, Pablo? Is it just you here? You mentioned your family."

"Only me. For now. I was going to be married, but she moved back to Oaxaca City. She didn't like the beach. And my parents . . . they're dead."

Ruggy nodded once and crossed his arms again.

"But look at what you have," he said, "you can make any life you want."

Pablo knew this was his other gift: his freedom to welcome strangers into his home, serve them beer, marijuana, play records for them, sometimes serenade them under the dried palm leaves in good weather and bad. This was when the Bungalows came to life, and he loved to see it as his father had intended—full of exotic travelers. Yet, in those festive times, as Pablo watched them all leave to either go back to their rooms when a storm scared them away, or to check out for the season, he knew he'd be alone again, but at home. The only place he knew.

"True," Pablo said. "I think about that because I know it can all change one day. That it will change."

"You're deep, man," Ruggy said.

Pablo shrugged and went back to setting up the patio. A couple other guests began to arrive, finding a place to sit, pulling cigarettes out for a morning smoke. Jucélia had appeared, peeking in, and looking somewhat defeated to see Ruggy already there. He went for her, as usual it seemed, to claim her.

"Coffee?" Pablo offered to Jucélia.

"Yes, please." She moved forward, away from Ruggy.

"I already asked him," Ruggy said.

"What?" Jucélia stood at the table where Pablo had set a steaming pot of coffee with an assortment of cups, cream, and sugar.

"He's not playing at the bar tonight," Ruggy said. "The girls loved that so much, they wanted to see you again."

"Thank you," Pablo said. "But no, not tonight at La Sirena."

"That's fine," Jucélia said. "We'll find something to do." She smiled but lost it once Ruggy had taken her hand.

"Let's go back to the room," he said, kissing her neck.

"We'll see you, Pablo," Ruggy said, and the two left.

8 - FAITH

"SHE LOVED YOU SO MUCH," Marcos says. "She wrote all of herself into this story. But now how did it end between you? She gave you the book, and then what? Did it just end?"

"After our weekend in Ensenada, I knew it would be different. We were changing. It was a way of saying goodbye. She was going for more school in California. She said she was moving on from her family and wanted to start new. Later that year, I quit walking the zócalo. I had saved up enough money to earn a teaching certificate and went to work at the Instituto. I later met Teresa."

"And then you and Joanne lost touch?"

"We wrote a few letters here and there, but over time, they died out. In one of her last ones, she had begun her teaching program and I understood that she was surrounded by smart people like her. She mentioned a mentor, a professor, she liked working with. I assumed maybe they were together. And of course, she mentioned her family. Her father disliked that she moved to California and said if she ever went back to Mexico—*filthy* Mexico, he had called it—she would never be welcome in their family. I realized then that we were different people from different cultures and not meant to be together. After a while, that part of my life was dead to me."

"Until it wasn't," Marcos says.

"You're right." I laugh. "It came back to life in those days, as you remember, during my sabbatical. My son knew I wanted—that I needed—something more in my life. He spent hours on his computer looking for jobs for me. 'You're going to need a visa,' he said, 'It will take time.'

"When I had time alone with his computer, I continued to search on my own. I was curious about this religious center I found when I first read the name McCasey. There was a site for a Christian ministry, and they were looking for artists and teachers. It felt forbidden to be exploring it because what if it was Joanne's husband's business, and there I was making plans in my head to maybe go there, to intrude in their holy life. But the place looked quite beautiful.

"I showed Felipe, and he was dumbfounded.

"'What is this? How did you hear about this?'

"I could not tell if he was happy or angry with me. As he clicked through the site, his face brightened like he had just discovered a new paradise. It helped that Felipe was faithful. One of the many wonderful gifts he received from Teresa was devotion to God. It's a strange mystery how this takes hold in some people and not in others."

"Or how it comes and goes," Marcos says. "I feel like I'm losing mine."

"I don't know if I ever had mine, but sometimes it creeps back in. Whatever it is, it's there and then it isn't. For Felipe, it was always there. His home was like my Tía Adelina's home. Saints and crosses everywhere. I appreciate his faith. It will be good for my grandson. And so, this is why Felipe felt more at ease looking at this place on the internet. It was like no other place I've ever seen. Sand-colored buildings with tall glass windows, marble floors inside, palm trees, fountains—it was like a movie set had been cut away and placed there next to the highway in between malls and restaurants.

"And there was a village. The International Village. This was the centerpiece of the entire place. It was built to look like a long cobblestone street with plazas and booths. They were trying to replicate a busy bazaar with merchants, shopkeepers, food—they wanted the smells and sounds to be perfect. That's what the whole place was, a perfect replica of something else. There were sections to show different parts of the world, and so there was a Latin American section. That's where I came in.

"On the jobs page of the site, it said they were looking for artisans and craftsman from different countries. In the Latin American village, they needed a potter who was an expert in clay and kiln work, and it showed a full shop with a place to give classes. Felipe knew I was excited when I saw this. He looked further into it and saw that all the workers would have housing and meals. The center would provide uniforms to represent the native clothing of that region. All I had to do was arrive. He felt safer about it all. I told him he could visit one day. I made a deal with him then that I would try it for six months. A J-1 visa had its limits anyway. I would be able to work there as long as there was a job for me.

"It took months to get the visa. During that time, Felipe changed my diet, made me walk and swim. He took me to the doctor for my physical—part of the job requirement—he had my eyes and blood checked, and he took me shopping, even though I didn't need to bring any special clothes or shoes.

"'Who knows what they're going to dress you like,' he said. 'It sounds more like a museum than a real village.'

"He was doubtful. Teresa was like that. She didn't trust people and businesses the way I did. I always put faith in people, that they would do the best by you if you did the best by them. That's what my father had taught me when we sold candy on the streets.

"Once I had my visa, Felipe made a flight reservation for me.

"'One way,' he said. 'For now. Don't get any ideas to stay there.'

"From Oaxaca to Mexico, then onto San Diego, I admit I felt like a little boy. Especially the way Felipe and his family left me at the airport—you'd think they were never going to see me again. Looking back, maybe they were right to cry and hug me the way they did. When I arrived in San Diego, it was like arriving on another planet. Everything zipped and whizzed by, and nothing was out of place or broken. There was almost no smell of anything. No cracks or bumps or dust and dirt, just sun and sky and faces that seemed to smile, but behind their eyes there was desperation and exhaustion. The place made me tired, and I hadn't even left the airport.

"At the bottom of the escalator, a young man held a sign for the Faith Mission World Center. FMWC. He smiled at me, his face and head beaming, like an angel.

"'Welcome home,' he said, then switched to Spanish.

"Other than a black backpack, the clothes and shoes I wore was all I had. There was no need to wait for luggage. When the young man ushered me to a group of other people, the other recent arrivals, I had a flash of fear: *what am I doing here? Who are these people? Is this safe?* I had a sense of something wrong about all of it, but I pushed that out of my head knowing I was going to a house of God. That it was all for good.

"My fear went away once I arrived and realized the place was better than the pictures. It was a true paradise. Everything sparkled it was so new and clean, and it didn't feel like a religious place since there were no crosses or statues of Jesus or the saints. All of the art was modern with shapes and colors, or that of nature with scenes of beautiful oceans and horizons. The only thing that seemed out of the ordinary was the constant sound of the freeway in the background, like a quiet but steady wind.

"At the orientation of the workers, I understood how big the operation was. We sat in the endless pews of the main chapel—a long hall with tall windows at the altar capped with a round globe-like dome. After interpreters handed out earpieces for all the different languages spoken, the program begin. The various directors spoke about their departments and expectations. Cleanliness was number one. That was repeated by all of them. Smiling and making pilgrims feel welcome and safe was after cleanliness. Pilgrims was the word they used for guests. And most importantly, chapel service every Wednesday for all staff, and a second chapel service for permanent staff every Saturday evening. That's what I was: permanent staff. As in those who lived there.

"As the department directors spoke, they blended the ideas of work and God and added prayers in between. It was then I became impatient. I wanted to settle in and start working, but knowing that I was in San Diego, I also wanted to find what I came to find. Joanne.

"As the orientation came to a close, they introduced the leaders. I thought I might hear the name McCasey, yet there was no mention of it. The founder, however, a tall, suited man named Peter O'Connor took the pulpit. He prayed over us, invoked God, and he paced around as he did it. He looked up often and closed his eyes. I had never seen anything like that. I only knew men of God to stand at the front of a church serious and somber, like they were religious robots. This—this was, I don't know: both exciting and scary.

"Many people shouted back at him, their hands up or arms waving, agreeing with him, telling him he was right. Others, like me, sat and watched, waited for it to be over. When it was, I was relieved. I wanted him to stop preaching. If it was meant to turn me to this religion, O'Connor was a good persuader, but not for me. I could see he took more pride in the place than he did in his religion. That was most of what he talked about. It was their grand opening, so I can see why he was passionate, yet it reminded me to keep my work separate from any feelings they were trying to put inside of us.

"Settling in was fast, especially when you bring nothing. We were assigned dormitories and a roommate. Again, nothing I had ever done, and it's funny how now, at the end of my life, I was doing all the things only young men do: leave the country, have roommates, and chase impossible women. My roommate was José, a woodworker from Zacatecas. Aside from him being ten or so years younger than me and much more sociable, he had a similar background. He was an art instructor in Mexico and wanted to work in the United States for a while. He had family in San Diego and knew people. He seemed connected already, and it helped that he was religious. He had some of that happy glow the American workers there had, as though they were injected with the Holy Spirit so that it made them smile and shine all the time.

"But José was also real, and a fellow countryman, so we got along well. We related to the sterile foreignness of the place and wished often just to have a scent of tacos al pastor. There were other men too that had traveled far with their trades and skills carrying their J-1 visas. Our holy papers, we joked. Agustín was a weaver from Guatemala, and Salomón, a painter from Columbia. We became friends quickly and started a new little life together innocent as children.

"The food in the cafeteria was delicious and plentiful. Not a tortilla in sight, but always something nutritious. And lots of fruits and vegetables. After a week, however, I learned the pattern. Sunday was a roast, Monday vegetarian, Tuesday pork chops, Wednesday Italian, Thursday chicken, Friday fish, and Saturday hamburgers. I had no reason to complain. There was shelter, food, and people around me. Everything was safe and comfortable.

"Hundreds of people came to the grand opening of the mission and village. The artisans, as we were called, simply stood in our studios and workspaces and greeted people as they came through. The television reporters were there with their cameras and other official-looking people. We were told to smile and if asked anything, only say how happy we were to be there.

"There were also protesters. They opposed Peter O'Connor and his views about religion, abortion, who could love whom.

"'Don't pay attention to any of that,' the ministers said, 'focus on your work, the pilgrims, and our mission.'

"The protesters came and went. Sometimes there were many there, and other times there were none. They stood at the entrance, so we in the village rarely saw them. We only saw the pilgrims—the people looking for something to do with their hands. They were people who came for God and stayed to make or buy something. I realized early on that the village and the shops and classes were how they intended to make their money and we were their salespeople; we were the ones whose job was to keep the pilgrims happy and entertained.

"At the grand opening and the many days that followed, the days that were the most crowded, I kept thinking Joanne might show up. I was certain she would walk through with the groups of well-dressed important people. *She had to be part of the mission*, I thought. But there were so many people those days, plus, the real work of doing our crafts, had begun. I didn't have much time to be on a constant watch for her. I looked up often when groups of people peeked in my potter's shop. I studied the older women that came through just to look around but not take a class. I had two images in my head: the girl I last saw in Ensenada so many years ago, and the woman from the website—the adult that the girl had become. I had to let go of the young Joanne when I looked for her in the crowds. Either way, I never saw her.

"After the crowds, the work began, and the days began to blend together. The classes were simple. Not much like what I taught at the Instituto in Oaxaca where the students came for weeks at a time. At the Mission, people came for a day or two at the most, or some just an afternoon. They made the basic things like bowls and vases. Almost everyone made simple crosses that I baked in the kiln for them to pick up the next day. Many people just wanted to watch me work, as though I was the attraction. The other workers and I joked about this at night back in the dorms, how we were like talented zoo animals.

"Every two weeks or so, Felipe and I spoke on the phone.

"'How is it?' he asked. 'Are you safe? Are you eating?'

"As if I was a child wandering the street. 'Yes, yes, I told him. Everything is fine. I love my job.'

"I told him he didn't need to call as often. He said I should write to him using e-mail, said he wanted to send me pictures that way, but I rarely used the computer in the employee room. Only the phone. I didn't want more complications.

"'Well, then you call me,' Felipe said. 'We're happy to know that you're safe and enjoying it. We love you. I love you. I miss you.'

'I miss you, too.'

"I missed them, but I liked where I was and what I was doing, and sometimes I forgot why I had come in the first place. That was the simple beauty of work, to get lost in the act of what you were doing so not to worry about everything else. And there was plenty of work. When it was slow in our workshops, they had us do chores around the village. Small things like sweep and pick up trash. It was all voluntary at first, then they started to assign extra jobs. More cleaning and kitchen work. Work in the sanctuary and office buildings."

"So they were preparing you for here?" Marcos smiles.

"It began to feel like—not what we were hired to do. But that was because the interest in the classes had fallen."

"Still, they shouldn't have turned you into the janitors," Marcos said. "Did they make the other international people sweep and mop? Did you ever see Asian or African people do that type of work?"

"As I think of it, no, not many. Maybe more of the black people."

"You see what I mean? They say it's not about the color of your skin, but it always is."

"Well, and that's why the protesters came again. José, my roommate, you remember, was a mover. He was smart and knew people inside and had family and friends in town. He never said it to us, never admitted that he did this, but as the reporters began to show up again, and although we didn't know they were reporters, and neither did the Mission, José talked to them. They came to ask us about our jobs. The activists came into the village, too, and the Mission leaders tried to stop it, but the news was out. Before long, the crowds were back at the Mission, and they weren't the ones happy to see it open.

"The Mission leaders kept the main entrance closed to protesters, so they stayed near the large fountain in the front driveway holding their signs and shouting. Peter O'Connor had told the whole staff during one of our mandatory chapel times there was nothing to worry about.

"'Keep calm, keep your head held high, and serve the Lord,' he said.

"There was a rumor going around that he was caught in some controversy himself, that he had made some remarks about same-sex marriage. I never realized how California was as a society—that anything goes. Seems like that's why everyone comes, no? Well, Peter O'Connor was one of them, too. He was an outsider. He had brought his beliefs from somewhere else in the United States, the South I had heard.

"The protesters didn't back away. They came in the morning, afternoon, and at night. The visitors to the Mission dropped to almost nothing. We had very little work to do. Each night, everyone returned to the living quarters on the back lot whispering with worry. Could the city shut it down just because of the violence it had created? Wasn't this a place for good? For God?

"Talk of the city shutting it down got into my head. I talked with José one night since he knew more about the situation.

"'What will happen?' I asked him.

"'I heard they might close the village. I also heard they might close the whole place. Peter O'Connor is not well-liked in San Diego. The mission was not welcome from the beginning. Here in the United States, there are two groups of people. Two kinds of politics. That's what this fight is about.'

"'And the city? Are they going to decide?'

"'It's possible. If the protests and complaints about O'Connor continue, the City Council can decide with the Mayor.'

"Over the next two weeks, everything would change. It was like that part in the bible, when Noah is building the arc. Something was going to happen. The sky could start pouring rain any minute. Peter O'Connor was caught using a secret identity on one of the dating services through your phone—one of the apps, I don't remember which one, but the details of his use of it were terrible. He had created a personality to ask for sex with young women. He got caught when one came forward to the news media.

"After that, the protests that were originally for the workers' rights grew into protests against O'Connor and for the protection of women. Everyone was screaming about something. O'Connor denied that he had done anything and said that he was set up because no one liked the Faith Mission World Center. He went on TV and cried. When I saw that, I knew it was over. I realized then exactly what the Faith Mission World Center was—artificial. It was indeed a zoo, and we were the animals.

"Soon after, the City decided to close parts of the Center, the International Village was the first to go. There was too much liability to keep it open. The managers left us without options when they started cutting staff. They said our visas would be null and void within a month, and that it would be better if we made our way *home* on our own. How they talked—null and void—using extra words to make their point.

"During those days of cleaning up our workstations and emptying what little we had of our personal belongings in our dormitories, a panic set in. I knew I had to call Felipe and tell him what happened, and I knew he would fly me back home to Oaxaca immediately and everything would be fine, but I felt defeated. I had come all this way looking for something I might never find. I was mad at myself and scared. On one of the last night's at the Mission, José and I stayed up late talking. I said I needed help, that I couldn't leave the U.S. just yet.

"'I have relatives here. My brother-in-law's family. The Sanchez family,'" José said. "One of them runs restaurants here. Let me see if I can find you some work.'

"'Anything helps,' I told him.

"Thank God José had connections. The next day he gave me a phone number to Arturo Sanchez, manager at Sea of Cortez Mexifresh Cantina y Cocina.

"'They need kitchen workers at the one in Mission Valley,' José said. "It's near the World Center. You'll be in the back where it's safer.'

"José himself went to one of the locations near the beaches.

"Wait," Marcos says. "Mexifresh?"

"I know, it's a silly word. A gringo way of saying that it's fresh and Mexican. It's a popular restaurant. The story is that the founder brought the fish taco to the United States."

Marcos shrugs, then winces in pain again.

"It's not important. The good thing is I had a place to work while the visa was still valid, and José knew someone with an extra room to rent in a house south in San Ysidro, a mile or so from the border. He wrote the directions down and which trolley to take. The only trouble is I had a long commute. That's when I would read Joanne's book. It was the only thing that kept me going."

"Go back to her story," Marcos says. "That's what's keeping me going now, too."

Slip Soul by Joe DeVries
Chapter 3

The rest of the morning moved along and with it came the memories Pablo had been trying to stifle. Once he was with Tía Claudia and Jorge later that evening, after they had eaten Domingo and Eva Garza's favorite meal of mole rojo con pollo and prayed at the altar with their pictures surrounded by candles, all would be well, and then Pablo could move on into the rest of the year.

Pablo and his godmother chose the day of Eva's passing—Pablo's mother—to hold the vigil. That day felt right. Pablo had been there until the end with his mother, but with Pablo's father Domingo's disappearance, there never was a sense of closure. Both days were etched in Pablo's mind, and though he lost them apart from each other, time had blended their deaths into one event in his mind.

The morning Domingo was lost at sea, he pulled Pablo, who was playing in the garden, aside and pointed to the sun. Domingo still reeked of alcohol from the night before.

"You see that big circle around the sun?" The weather those days, typical of late summer, had been dry in the morning, then steamy in the afternoon and into the night.

Young Pablo held up his hand to shield his eyes. A thin hazy halo larger than any other ring he had ever imagined on any other distant planet encircled the bright sun. "Yes. What is it?"

"The weather is going to change soon. Now go tell your mother we're going to take the boat out before it does."

Pablo knew his mother would not like this. The night before was his Tío Luis's twenty-eighth birthday party, plus, they were celebrating, much to Pablo's mother's frustration, the grand opening of the then eight-room inn that would later be Los Bungalows de Las Brisas. Casa Garza, as it was first known, had been in full swing for about four months. His father kept saying how one day this would all be Pablo's, and one day, they will come by the thousands.

Eva and Domingo had another fight after the party. She hated the idea of trying to start a motel. For who, she had said. Who is going to come here? What are they going to see? Coffee? Iguanas?

She wanted another child, too, and made this well-known.

"Pablo will be old enough to be the boy's uncle by the time we have another one," she said. *Ándale.* Get on with it.

But Domingo Garza was busy, never short of a project with the Bungalows, and always in search of his next *conquista.*

After they had stopped yelling at each other, Pablo's father had brought the tequila out and got himself even more wasted, and then passed out on the couch. That next morning, he was up before anyone else, hard at work clearing some overgrown weeds near the shed. Pablo had found his father, drinking coffee and smoking a cigarette. It was then he sat Pablo down and showed him the corona around the sun.

"Papá says we're going sailing," he told his mother.

"No, we are not," Eva said. "Tell him he's still drunk."

Telling Domingo Garza that he was drunk, or worse, still drunk, was a quick way to start a fight. He wasn't a big man, but the fight in him was, and Pablo had witnessed his father bring down men bigger than him when he was challenged. It was almost always on a night of drinking.

Domingo appeared in the kitchen as Eva had said this and grabbed the fabric of her huipil and pulled her up, just enough off of the chair at the dining table.

"Get ready," Domingo said. "We're leaving now."

How men changed so fast from one feeling to the next, Pablo didn't know. His father could be happy and smiling one minute, then tense with anger the next. Pablo had been on the end of that physical rage often, his little body bearing the pain of a neck grab, a squeeze of the arm that left a mark, or a stinging slap to his behind.

Eva pushed back from the table in silence. She cleared the dishes, washed them as though nothing was wrong, wiping her hands on her apron, which she took off and hung on the hook by the crucifix. Domingo stood by and watched.

"Ten minutes," he said, and went back out to work.

Eva guided Pablo out of the kitchen and into the small washroom between the two bedrooms. She shut the door and leaned over him, her eyes frantic and welling with tears. She gripped his shoulders, held him still.

"Listen to me," she said. "Go to Tía Claudia's house. Now. Run. Stay there until I get back."

"No, *mami*, don't go."

"Do as I say, please. Your father's drunk. He needs to rest. Please, go."

At that time, Claudia hadn't moved up into the hills yet. She was Eva's only true friend, her sister in spirit, and she lived right in town.

Pablo did as he was told, but he lingered. He ducked around corners to watch his mother and father. They shouted, he grabbed her again. Pablo heard something about sending Pablo to play with Jorge. He stayed around long enough to watch his father lead his mother out to the beach where the catamarans were tied. They both pushed the boat down the slope of sand and got on. Above them, the sky had begun to turn hazy, and the breezes had picked up.

At Claudia's house, Pablo sat silent at her kitchen table, an uneaten plate of *chile rellenos* in front of him. He got up to peek out of the small window in her front room every few minutes, but Claudia would take him and walk him around her house, showing him things he'd seen hundreds of times. Her books, her shrine to the Virgin, her guitar.

"Let's light a candle," she said.

"It's too hot in here," he said.

"Here. Kneel. Have you been practicing your prayers? Come on. Ave Maria."

"I don't want to pray."

"Close your eyes."

Pablo went back to the small window.

"It's raining," he said.

Claudia went for Pablo, walked him back to the altar. "You can always pray to the Blessed Mother. She listens. She tells God. Come kneel."

He knew the prayer by heart. He and his mother said it every night. He liked the second part best. How the rhythm sounded like a little song. Except the part about death. *The hour of our death.* He had known about death. Insects, dogs, his *abuelos* a few years before. He didn't cry though. He didn't know then that it was final.

Santa Maria, Madre de Dios
Ruega por nosotros, pecadores
Ahora, y en la hora nuestra
Muerte.
Amen.
Amen.

Muerte. There's no other way than that.

He cried, eyes closed. They'd been saying the prayer over and over, Claudia holding him by her side. Claudia squeezed him and she began to cry with him.

"*Tía*? What's wrong?"

"Nothing," she said.

He had known about Claudias's visions. How his mother was always talking about how Claudia could *see* things before they happened. How her dreams told her things. Pablo's father waved his hand at that. *Basta!* She's thinks she's a witch, he would say. Don't believe any of that.

Outside, the rain fell harder. Domingo Garza was right about the weather. Claudia kept them praying, each citing of the plea was faster than the one before. The lights in her kitchen flickered. She went to turn them off, then grabbed two knives from the drawer. She flung open the front door and made a cross with the knives, held them up in front of her face. Rain drops hit her as she shouted the prayer into the sky.

Santa Maria, Madre de Dios
Ruega por nosotros, pecadores
Ahora, y en la hora nuestra
Muerte.
Amen.

"*Tía*, no!" Pablo went for her, clutched at her waist to pull her inside. She continued to pray, her words evaporating into the cool, wet air, a foggy mist growing around them. As another gust of wind blew against her whitewashed wall, a figure emanated from the thick, gray atmosphere. Holding herself, body shaking, her clothes drenched, Eva Garza stepped forward, face wet from the rain and tears streaking down.

"*Mami!*" Pablo ran to her, grabbed her into a hug so hard, he almost brought her down. Claudia dropped the knives to the wet ground and fell to her knees.

Inside, wrapped in a blanket, Eva drank some hot tea Claudia had made. Eva held Pablo and kissed him, told him to go lie down in Claudia's bedroom.

"I'm not tired," he said.

"Go."

Pablo left the kitchen, but stayed near, close enough for his ears to hear his mother tell Claudia everything. How they had launched the boat, how Domingo was like a crazy man, shouting orders, smelling like alcohol so bad you could squeeze it out of him. All she could do was obey him. She didn't want to be hit anymore. He calmed down once they were on smooth water, but then he opened a small bag he had brought, which had two bottles of beer. He opened one and stared to drink. The clouds, the rain, look, she kept saying. She knew she could make it back if she swam. The beach wasn't that far. He cursed, finishing his beer, held the sail tight in the direction of Bahía Principal.

Domingo turned away, and inside of her she felt something electric, like she had the power to kill something with her own hands, or that she could fly, or—like she was outside of her body somehow—and then, she jumped.

"All I could think about was Pablito," she said. She cried and Claudia took her hand.

"What about Domingo?" Adelina said.

"Bah," she said. "Let him go."

She laughed a little, and Claudia stopped her. Pablo's godmother tipped her head to the side. Pablo knew he'd been found. Eva called him over.

"*Hi'jito*, you're safe and that's all the matters."

"*Papá*?"

"He's—he needs to be alone sometimes. He'll be—" Eva stopped. "Did you eat?"

"I'm not hungry." Pablo went to the window again. "Storm's dying."

He felt bigger using a word like that to describe something ending. He wouldn't say that his parents' marriage was dying. They still slept together. Not like his cousin Jorge, who said his dad was always sleeping on the couch. Pablo's parents just yelled a lot, and his father got so mad he scared everyone. That was why Eva was always visiting Claudia. To get away from his temper.

The storm passed. No damage to the town. It was only another summer monsoon, not a hurricane. Those came once every few decades. Pablo had recently learned a decade was a period of ten years. It would take him more than two of those to make peace with what happened to his father that day, maybe fifty decades to want to go back into the water himself.

Late that afternoon, as the sun was dropping back into the ocean for the night, fishermen just south of Playa Zicatela had caught something big. There was a commotion on the beach and people ran down to see what it was. The catamaran had come to shore, the sail ripped from the jib. Cords had come undone. No pilot on the canvas either. Everyone knew it was Domingo Garza's boat by the name Eva painted on the right hull.

Over the next several weeks, Eva returned to her home only for clothes for her and Pablo. Beyond that, mother and son stayed at Claudia's house, where she fed them, prayed with them and over them, anointed them with her oils and herbs, and cast her own healing incantations. The funeral for Domingo was well attended and painful, with several of Domingo's friends, his brother Luis especially, doubtful Domingo was even dead. He's probably out there swimming, he had said, or maybe he washed up on an island. Or maybe Eva—well, no one knows exactly what happened on the boat. She says she swam back. But what happened before that? He had said.

Pablo watched his mother sob every night, nothing able to console her. She began coughing soon after, complaining of a sore throat. Claudia's teas and tinctures only did so much. Eva thought it best to keep Claudia in quarantine, having Pablo wear a bandana over his mouth and nose when he went in to see his mother.

When her joints began to ache several weeks later, Claudia called in a doctor, who said Eva needed medicine stronger than the strongest herbal remedy. He called her infection *la fiebre*. The rheumatic fever. Pablo began to complain of similar symptoms, but after careful examination, he had nothing. He was suffering from sympathy pain, with the memory of his father's death, though he didn't witness it, still fresh in his head.

While Eva rested, Claudia never let Pablo out of her sight. She taught him more prayers, how to breathe to calm himself, and played songs for him on her guitar. It was in those days that he began to take interest in the instrument. In the evenings, after they had fed Eva, Claudia took Pablo outside to show him the ocean. For the first few months, he refused to even look, but over time, she got him to at least walk on the fine black and yellow sand, his toes digging in, Claudia talking about all different things all at once, as though she was herself a little hysterical.

The summer turned to fall, and fall cooled into winter. Eva's heart only weakened further. She had made an agreement with Claudia that should anything happen to her, Claudia would become Pablo's guardian. Luis Garza said otherwise. He claimed his brother Domingo had made a pact with him long ago, that they would always help each other if the other one was in trouble.

The rounds of antibiotics took their toll on Eva, and Claudia's remedies didn't help. By that time, Pablo was about to start puberty, and his voice was beginning to crack. He wasn't a little boy anymore, and the last year had made him grow up even faster. He knew about Claudia and his Tío Luis, how they fought over him, but how they made up when he visited late at night.

When Eva was in her final days, Pablo became mad. He blamed her for not taking him too on the boat that day; said he could have talked to his father to turn back. Eva was too weak to argue and could only cry when Pablo wouldn't. She had said to him, "I miss the man I married a long time ago. I see him in you. I see me in you, too. You're both of us but be yourself. Be better than us."

The vigil for his parents started at sundown. Claudia had arrived and she had brought the food with her. Claudia was the closest Pablo had to a mother, and he hugged his madrina with all he had. Claudia, though turning frailer with age was still strong enough to return his love with more of hers. Jorge arrived with a bottle of mezcal, and Claudia quickly ordered him to put that away.

As night fell, they lit the candles at a small altar placed in the patio of Los Bungalows de Las Brisas with pictures of his parents next to them. After, they walked down to the ocean to drop marigolds in the sea. Pablo had brought his guitar and played a few songs.

Once their procession had returned to the Bungalows, several guests, including Jucélia, Renata, and Ruggy sat in the patio having their own *hora feliz*.

"Hey man, you didn't tell us you were having a party on the beach!" Ruggy shouted.

Jucélia elbowed Ruggy, pointing to the altar. She looked across at Pablo and apologized with downturned eyes, shaking her head just a bit, with her hand over her heart.

Slip Soul by Joe DeVries
Chapter 4

19 Agosto 1978
Day 3, Playa Zicatela

How to explain my emotions right now?
Scared.
Waiting.
Happiness (growing).

Scared because Lester hurt me, again. He takes my wrists and squeezes them and holds me up, my feet almost off the ground. His face is like a devil's with his eyes wide and the veins on his neck bulging and beating. When I try to look away, he grits his teeth and demands that I look at him, as though I was his child. As if he was discipling me. Thank God he cannot yell at me here at the Bungalows.

Tonight it was for the look I gave Pablo. Lester said I was flirting with him. I wasn't. I was only showing sympathy. It was the anniversary of his parents' death—how can I not have sympathy? He gave me a good bruise this time. It fades away soon though, and I can wear a long sleeve tomorrow.

Waiting. I'm waiting for this all to change. I know it will someday. I feel bad for thinking this because Lester has done so much for Renata and me, but I know he's wrong for me. And I know I should not be sitting around hoping and waiting for something to change. I should be making the change. Renata and me have dreams to go to the United States. She wants to be a nurse, and I want to be a teacher. I feel like we are halfway there here in Mexico.

And then happiness. Happiness because maybe this is where we—where I—am supposed to be. This place is beautiful. It's a paradise. The sun and the heat, the waves, the food. And ... I am finally saying it (because I know I have been feeling it), this happiness grows because of _____. The moment I saw him, I felt something inside of me. An instant connection. I cannot deny I felt it. I wonder if he did too.

This is what grows. It's like a little seed has been planted in a garden and it will take sun and water and time for it to flourish. It does not need much to make it grow. That is the miracle of this.

I have to stop for now. I hear Lester coming in.

9 - SEA OF CORTEZ MEXIFRESH CANTINA Y COCINA

MARCOS IS BEAMING WITH JOY as I read the story.

"I get it," he says. "Pablo's Tía Claudia is your Tía Adelina. And how Pablo's parents died? How his father drown at sea? He was so alone."

"And so was Jucélia."

"And the food. Chile rellenos. Mole," Marcos says. "I didn't realize I was starving. I would do anything for yucca con chicharrón and sopa de caracol. Food from my country."

"Oh, mole. That's all I want."

"Mexicans and your mole," Marcos says.

"Oaxaqueñoes and our mole."

We move on to the foundation for all our food—beans, rice, and tortillas—and how there's more in common with our plates amongst the countries than there are differences, and this makes us wish for them more. Just then, Nurse Vargas arrives with what is supposed to be lunch, but who knows what time of day it really is, and the arrival of food makes me realize we never had breakfast. They never served anything. Nurse Vargas sets down bologna sandwiches and cups of noodle soup. Marcos and I turn to each other, our eyes saying everything.

"Are you feeling better?" she asks, checking me first.

"Still sore and tired."

She moves over to Marcos and checks his pulse, puts her hand on his forehead. "Do you need more pain medication? You got it the worst."

Marcos nods, shrugs.

Vargas steps back to speak to both of us. She lowers her voice.

"These men here, these guards—you can't go around causing trouble. They will hurt you. They are trained to do that. They're all talking about what happened with you two. Lovato is definitely in trouble."

I nod to Marcos.

"But that doesn't mean you aren't. Your actions here have consequences. They can send you back just like that. I don't know what's going to happen when you're ready to go back into the detention area. Just be safe and don't cause any problems."

"How much time here?" Marcos says.

"I don't know. Another day maybe. Just rest. Eat," she says.

Marcos turns away from the food.

"I know, it's not good," she says, "I'll see what I can find."

Nurse Vargas walks out, and Marcos and I stare at the food.

"How am I supposed to eat this?" he says. "My arm is tied to me, and this one hurts to move."

"I would walk over there and feed you, but my leg is screaming."

We laugh again, and it's one of those fits that might turn to crying, when you feel yourself coming apart.

"She's nice anyway," Marcos says.

"Yes, but can you trust her? Can we trust her?"

"She's harmless."

"Something I learned here in the United States is that it's difficult to know who you can trust. I haven't told you much about the restaurant and my co-workers. One in particular. Daisy."

"Another girlfriend?" Marcos teases.

"No, man, stop it. She was, well, not what I expected. She's why I'm here."

"Not Joanne?"

"No, the reason I am here—in this detention center."

"What happened with her? And what was it like making Mexifresh—or what was it that you called it?"

"For one, at Sea of Cortez there wasn't a leader coming by all the time to check on you like there was at the Faith Mission World Center. Instead, Sea of Cortez, had these comic strips on the wall that showed how to make the food. Job aids, they called them. All the work areas at Sea of Cortez Mexifresh Cantina y Cocina had them, like the Stations of the Cross, but instead of Jesus falling to his knees, Corto the fat little gringo surfer with no teeth was the guide. Corto, the mascot, came on Monday nights when kids ate free.

"In front of my station, the signs said how to make the totopos.

Step 1. Dump fried chips into warmer drawer

Step 2. Squeeze bottled lime juice onto hot chips

Step 3. Shake salt generously over chips

Step 4. One scoop of chips per wicker basket (make sure basket is lined)

"The work was so easy it was torture, same with dropping the cut corn tortillas into the fryer and setting the timer. Pinche Tomás was proud to demonstrate a generous shake of salt.

"On my first day at work, manager Arturo Sanchez explained why they called Pinche Tomás, Pinche Tomás: 'Salt can make anyone a chef,' he said.

"The food there was . . . an imitation. Nothing like home. No tacos al pastor. No elotes, no tortas and the salt. Dios mío. The totopos were like a mouthful of sea water. And no, they're called chips, Daisy reminded me all the time.

"'They're chips, Valdo,' she said. "Chips, chips, chips."

"She was nice about it. She smiled and laughed. Not like Ernesto who worked the register when Daisy wasn't there. He was Mexicano, too, but proud of his English. He said chips so perfectly. Chips. Not cheeps. He said it to me once, on a busy day, like he was trying to give me some advice. He wanted to teach the old man something, that 'When you say cheeps, it sounds like cheap. Barato, you understand, don't you?'

"I forgave him for being un mocoso. With his wavy hair and how he held his shoulders back when he walked reminded me of a child trying to be a grown man, but not a gentleman. That's one thing Teresa and I made sure of, that Felipe would grow up to be a good man. She taught him to be kind to everyone. She raised a gentleman.

"The uniform at Sea of Cortez was a red guayabera shirt and tan pants, much better than the peasant clothes of the international village, but I never knew why they made the place feel tropical by playing Caribbean music and decorating it with parrots if it was a Mexican restaurant. But like so much in America, is anything what it's supposed to be?

"I spent most of my time in the kitchen, frying the totopos and preparing small meals like salads and kids' meals, then sliding them through an opening to the front counter. This work felt like my last act, one more stage to perform on while I ran out of days, before my holy paper expired, and before I would be a fugitive.

"'Totopos.' I would say, pushing baskets through.

"Daisy turned back. 'Chips.'

"'Cheeps,' I said.

"'Sounds like sheeps. ¿Como se dice sheep?'

"'Oveja,' I told her.

"Daisy practiced her Spanish all day. Some people called themselves Mexican, others, Mexican-American and some Latino. She called herself Hispanic. A wild thought planted itself in my head in those early days of knowing her, looking at her face, her mix of colors. That maybe she was the product of that last meeting in Ensenada with Joanne, when our relationship, which up until that point had only felt like a cool and distant romance, had at last changed in a few moments to the physical love we had avoided for so long. It was foolish to think that—to think I might be Daisy's father. It's what we dreamers do. Plus, she had told me about her grandparents—her mother's parents—who were from Rosarito.

"Daisy took orders, people's money, and on busy days, called them to the counter when their food was ready. When we were not busy, I sometimes carried the food out. Otherwise, I heard her voice often:

"'Welcome to Sea of Cortez Mexifresh Cantina y Cocina. M'help you?'

"'Simon, your order's ready. Simon?'

"When she was not taking orders, she always looked into our world curious to know about us. Pinche Tomás didn't say much. His English wasn't good. He had told me she was new, too. She had only started a few days before me. He once whispered to me that he didn't trust her.

"Between our worlds, the metal passageway warmed by the amber heat lamps, she looked at me sometimes with innocence and other times like she was trying to see more of me. Once, her eyes moved up and down, almost like the women that met me on the zócalo. She didn't see the once trim man with thick black hair. Only a big stomach, a rounded face, and above my high sweaty forehead was the remaining wave of my hair pressed into the paper cook's hat. Tío Miguel Ángel used dabs of pomade to paste my hair down that first night we went out onto the zócalo, licking his fingers and pressing down the stray hairs that resisted.

"Daisy wanted to talk all the time. She asked a lot of questions, and sometimes I thought she might be writing her own book. I think because she was young and seemed innocent, I trusted her, and so I told her why I was here. I told her what I told you. About Joanne, my past. Everything."

"Everything?" Marcos manages a bite of his sandwich.

"Well, almost everything. I told her about the trip to Zicatela, when Joanne and me visited Adelina. Daisy asked if I still did drugs. I was shocked by this. I told her no and explained that Joanne was writing a book. This interested her and she pressed me for more. "

"'It's a love story of a Brazilian girl and a Mexican man.' I told her. 'The man travels in his sleep.'

"'So what happened? Did she finish the book? Did you keep in touch?'

"'Mira. Es nueve,' I would tell her at closing time. 'Time to clean.' We closed together every night.

"'You're not telling me everything,' she said.

"Pinche Tómas finished the customers' orders. He flipped on the TV and switched the tropical Latin music to a Mexican pop station.

"A woman's to-go order was ready. Baja Chicken Burrito, no sauce, extra cheese, and two Junior Captain meals. A green field with tiny players running toward the tended goal flashed on the screen in the kitchen. It was a

European match: Barca versus Lisbon. Daisy called the woman up and handed her the bag of food. The lady and her two children left the restaurant.

"'That's it, mi linda. Ella se fue.'

"At least five more baskets-worth rested in the chip drawer. Artie Sanchez let us take as many home as we liked. Two bags for Daisy, two bags for Pinche Tómas, one for the house where I stayed, though often no one ate them. Next, I took the big bowls from the salsa bar, and dumped them back in the vats. The chipotle was the best one. The others were like water.

"Daisy locked the front door and pulled the string on the surfboard-shaped neon sign that said Bienvenidos. She moved on to the counters and tables, wiping them fast.

"'Do you want a ride home?' She asked me every night. 'You can tell me the rest of the story since you're too scared to tell it here.'

"'Ay, Daisy, no. No gracias,' I said to her every night. It was a matter of pride, and the dread of going to the place that was not home, but a room in a house full of extraños. All of them in between worlds, stuck at the border of their next phase in life. The young Mexican lady and her little girl, they seemed nice. She said hello once. The quiet man always with his head down—was too mean-looking to approach. Never did they leave a note of thanks for the chips when they did eat them, not like how my students did in Oaxaca City at the end of the term. *'Gracias, Señor Reyes!'*

"'Where do you live anyway?" she asked.

"'San Ysidro," I told her.

"'Shoot, you're so close to the border, you could just walk back to Mexico.'

"'I can,' I said. 'It's almost time for me to leave anyway.'

"'What do you mean?' she said.

"When Artie Sanchez hired me, he knew I only had a couple of weeks left on my visa, and he said to keep it quiet. In that moment with Daisy I tried to laugh it off.

"'Oh, nothing,' I said. 'You're right, you're right. I'm so close to home.'

"After that, I felt like I had to be careful around Daisy, be extra nice to her. Like I had to treat her like a client. There was a certain amount of nervousness I always felt with the women I served, and it suddenly became like that with Daisy.

"As the days went on, I knew something was bothering her, too. Some nights when we worked together but didn't close, we would eat a meal after clocking out. Sitting out on the patio one evening, I asked her, 'Are you tired?'

"Miguel Ángel said that women ask the questions and men do the talking. With Teresa, I learned how to ask questions without asking. If you're tired, let me know if I can do anything for you, instead of *are you tired?* I sometimes wondered if she disliked that I was so attentive, that she may have thought I never broke my habits as a zócalo boy.

"'Just a lot on my mind.' Daisy looked down at her food, closed her eyes and breathed in. I thought she was praying.

"'Your test?' She had told me she was in a teaching program and had a lot of studies.

"'Yes, that and other things.' She picked up her taquito and bit into it. She avoided my eyes that night, looked away, off toward the highway that ran nearby.

"'Buena suerte,' I said. 'You will do fine.'

"'You were a teacher,' she said. 'Did you like it?'

"'I loved it.'

"'Better than working the zócalo?' she said.

"I took a bite of my food. I had no reply. She wasn't herself.

"'I'm sorry. It's just—I don't know if I'm going to become a . . . teacher.'

"'Why not?'

"'It's um—my dad. He says he's not going to pay for my school anymore. He wants me to get a better paying job.'

"'You make money teaching.'

"'That's not what he says. And it's true. Teachers don't make much money. He wants me to go into law enforcement. He says I can work anywhere as a woman, and since I know some Spanish, he says I'll have better chances.'

"'The police?'

"She set her taquito down and finally looked at me.

"'ICE.'

"I knew by the look on her face she didn't mean what goes into the sodas.

"'Immigration,' she said.

"That word, like all those other things that made my guts turn inside out—Teresa, Joanne, Felipe, Puerto Escondido, Oaxaca—that one had a stronger punch. Especially then, with my visa days away from running out. It was a word that sat in the dark waiting for me, waiting to end my dream.

"'La 'migra?'

"'Yeah,' She finished her taquito, wiped her lips with a napkin. She looked torn inside. She had never said it to me, but I knew she was confused about herself, whether she was Mexican or American, or both. She had said her Dad was white, and that she said she *identified* more with her mother, her Mexican side. How she called them sides, as though there were two people in one body—I knew that feeling, too. The old me, the older me.

"'You can be manager here,' I said.

"'No, Valdo. This is only temporary. I don't want to manage a restaurant. My dad is right. I could work for Border Patrol and make triple what I make here, way more than a teacher.'

"'Not what you want.'

"'I don't know.' She looked at me, then away again. 'I don't know what I want.'

"Her profile reminded me of Joanne, how she would look off into the horizon, thinking about who knows what. With Teresa, there was no guessing. Either her words or her face said what was on her mind. With Joanne—like I found with Daisy—storms of all kinds raged on the inside, and yet there was no sign of it in their eyes.

"'You're so brave.' Daisy turned back to me. 'Coming here all by yourself. You must really be in love.'

"That hit me even harder. Young people know so much. Or maybe I showed too much. I couldn't pretend like I used to. Not like Juan De Ortega, the old me. A silence moved over us, and I tried to fill it like I did when a sense of awkwardness came between me and a client, but I had no words.

"She pulled out her phone. 'What was your girlfriend's name? Joanne McCasey?'

"'Watson. Joanne Watson McCasey.' How fast Daisy changed the subject was troubling, but in seconds, she had found pictures and pages about her—more than I ever found using Felipe's computer back home.

"'You said she was writing a book, right?' Daisy said. "Look.'

"Glowing on the screen of her phone was a book cover entitled *To Live Alive*. By Joanne McCasey Watson. I almost fell out of my chair.

"'Is this her?' Daisy asked. Before I could respond, she kept going on. 'It says it's about surviving abuse. Wow, hard life? Look, she has a new book coming out soon. It says her first collection of stories. And look! She has a reading next Friday night.'

"Ah, so she did publish the book," Marcos says. "Did you show Daisy you had the original version from Joanne?" Marcos points to the stack of papers I've been protecting.

"Oh, no, it was too private. In that moment, I felt like I had to go hide. Knowing Daisy might be joining Immigration and Customs, that Joanne had a book, and that she was reading soon hit me too hard."

"Then Daisy said, 'I'll take you on Friday.'

"What did you do?" Marcos says.

"Her phone rang, and her mood changed as she got up to take the call. Then she left. I felt relieved to be alone, to take the trolley back to my place in San Ysidro. I read the book on the way back, but I was distracted. I needed to think about what to do next.

"Eat, Marcos." I point to the food.

"I don't want it. But you can keep reading."

"I have to eat sometime, too."

"Not that. Starve a little bit and they will bring something better. So what happens next to Pablo?"

I sip the hot salty chicken broth and go back to Joanne's pages.

Slip Soul by Joe DeVries
Chapter 5

On the few stormy nights in Playa Zicatela, Pablo would sit alone on the patio under the palapa absorbed by the howling winds clashing with the roaring ocean. There were two distinct energies in battle, some only a skirmish to be settled in an hour or two, others a full-scale war resolved after a few days. The sheer power terrified and fascinated him. His only way to makes sense of *una tormenta* was to face them, live inside them.

Like the year his parents' had passed, the clouds began to gather again that August, and with that, Pablo decided to have a hurricane party at the Bungalows. Years before, Pablo never would have thought about something like that. When he was young, he had developed a phobia for storms, and he had even quit surfing.

Tía Claudia had helped him get over his fears walking him along the *malecón* in rainstorms, then bringing him back to La Casa Garza to sit on the patio to listen to the winds. With the palm trees bending, the palapa threatening to blow away, and the lanterns flickering, they would sit, side by side in wicker chairs or at a table, she talking to him about other things: what he was learning in school, were there any girls that he wanted to talk to, did he want to learn how to cook. Or they would play games. Loteria. Jacks. Cards.

"Storms will always come," she said, "and they always go. They will never take you away."

She had told him how massive typhoons are born in the South Pacific when warm and cold air meet, and how they travel across the ocean and swell into hurricanes that can hit the Pacific coast of Mexico. She called the coast *una cadera*—she was always comparing things to women's body parts. The belly button of América Centrál, the neck of the desert, the mountains of Mexico, rising like the breast of a woman.

As he grew up and learned to face the storms alone, Pablo brought his *novias* under the palapa, too, and they would nuzzle him, beg him to go inside. Why, why, why do we have to stay out here?

His last girlfriend, Olga, had to pull him inside the lobby once. They had talked about getting married. Her dream included a big church wedding in Oaxaca City, where her family would be moving back to soon. Puerto Escondido was changing, they had said. It was time to move on. That one storm had been the test for their relationship. Olga failed. He couldn't leave. The ocean and its violent storms were in his blood.

Over time, as the management of the hotel went from his uncles to him, after he'd renamed it Los Bungalows de las Brisas, he invited the guests out for parties. They'd drink beer and smoke joints, crank up Marley and the Eagles while the rain dripped through the roof.

Tonight, guests opened bottles of beer and began to huddle together as the storm came in. Jucélia, Renata, and Ruggy were among the ones that seemed puzzled that this was the time to have a party.

"This is a small one," Pablo assured them all. "Not to worry."

With the music blending with the whistling wind, food distracting them from the drop in temperature, and a few bottles of mezcal going around, the guests had relaxed. He went around checking on everyone—his nature being to provide for people. He came around to the trio.

"Everyone having fun?" Pablo said.

"It's beautiful out here," Renata said.

Jucélia, held by Ruggy, nodded in agreement.

"We like it so much here," Ruggy said, "we think we might stay."

"Oh?" Pablo said. "For how long?"

"Who knows," Ruggy said.

The rain fell harder. Pablo turned his attention to the ocean.

"Ruggy, will you help me move these sandbags? Just to be safe."

The two left the patio and walked along the tiled pathway that led to the *malecón*. A small slope from the street to the lobby door meant rain could pour into the property as it had done before.

"Here, take these and stack them," Pablo shouted over the rain, tossing the heavy bags to Ruggy.

"I thought you said it was a small storm?" Ruggy said.

"Yes, but you never know. So you want to stay here? To move here?"

"I have an idea. Want to hear it?"

"What's the idea?" Pablo stopped passing the bags to look up at Ruggy.

"I want to open a bar. Here on the beach," Ruggy said.

Pablo smiled, but he was confused. *How? Where?*

"Tell me more, after this," Pablo continued passing the bags, and Ruggy stacked. "There," he said. "Let's go back to the party."

Back under the palapa, the two stood soaking wet, sharing a laugh. Pablo offered Ruggy a beer, and he took it, but Ruggy began talking fast, raising his hands up, pointing out to the beach. From the corner of his eye, Pablo saw the girls standing across the palapa, their faces a combination of curiosity and concern.

Slip Soul by Joe DeVries
Chapter 6

20 Agosto 1978
Day 3, Playa Zicatela

Oh, P— I worry. I worry about what Ruggy is telling

you. He's been telling us the same thing since we arrived. He imagines a bar on the beach covered in palm leaves like the palapa here at your motel. He wants to have parties and women and ... he wants what you have. I believe he's jealous of you. How easy your life looks. He admires your peaceful nature because he can never have it. He can never be like you.

You have something special, P—. It's a feitiço—a power you have. He sees this in you—that charm you have, but he's a coward, and he knows it. He ran from the United States. He'll never tell you he was drafted for Vietnam, but he ran, fled to Brazil. He's damaged. He was abused and is now he's an abuser. It's a cycle. His father was in the Korean War. Lester has that in him. He thinks everything is a battle and yet he can't confront anything. Maybe that's why he likes la lucha: *because it's not real.*

He pulled you aside and I knew what he was doing. He was talking you into his idea. He does that. He manipulates people. It's how he got me and Renata. He came to the medical clinic where we worked in São Paulo needing bandages or something. There he was, this big Americano who said he was recovering from a fight, said he wanted to study jujitsu and capoeira in Brazil. He talked about repairing himself and slowing down, learning meditation. I don't know what I saw in him, other than he seemed innocent somehow, a little fragile, too. I wanted to help everyone then. It was in my nature, too. Renata liked him too. But that's another story.

But P—, please don't fall for his tricks. He can hurt you. He doesn't know the real you. I feel like I know the real you. I see you inside there. There's a lonely, sweet man in there. You have real emotions, and you care for people, and you understand how to care for others. I saw how you sing on that small stage, how you put your whole heart into it. It's like you're singing to one person.

I understand what you're going through. I feel your

pain. I want to help you how you help me. The funny thing, you don't know how you're helping me. You're helping me by just being who you are. All I can do is watch you from afar, and that's all I need.

And yet ... I'm starting to imagine more. About you. About me. Us.

10 - SAN YSIDRO

"TÍO," MARCOS SAYS. "THIS IS GETTING good. They're falling in love. But that damn gringo is in their way."

"That happens. They're everywhere."

"I wouldn't know. I haven't even been to the other side, really," Marcos says. "Of this country, I only know this place."

"That makes me sad for you. There are some nice places. They can't complain for what they have here. Even where I stayed in San Ysdiro, probably very close to here, was good, but everyone spoke badly of it. That's what I learned about the United States, you never knew what or who was good or bad. There, in San Ysidro, I stayed in a decent house and in a quiet neighborhood. In the mornings, the sun shined through haze, a combination of thick ocean air from the night before mixed with a brown band of pollution where the two countries met. Some days you could see the big flag of Mexico fluttering on the Tijuana side, other days you couldn't.

"Up the street, a homeowner had turned their driveway into a shrine of the Virgen de Guadalupe. They'd laced small lights around a trellis that protected her. A nearby church had daily mass in Spanish. Closer to the boulevard, there were casas de cambio, mercados, a bar, places to buy car insurance, and a motel. It's American in every way—the way it looks and feels, but everyone speaks Spanish. The town is a small body part of Mexico—the tip of a finger or a toe—just in the doorway of the United States. Or was it the other way around?

"La Bodega López, a few blocks further up, felt the closest to home. The owners, Hugo and Beatriz López from Michoacán had been in the States for almost twenty years. They were older, though they seemed young. Their shop had everything: soap and shampoo, milk, sliced cheese, ham, eggs, bananas, avocado, orange juice, and corn tortillas. Their tortillas were from a tortilleria. Many of the labels were strange American names, though there were plenty of familiar Mexican brands, like the dulces from my childhood. Those labels hadn't changed.

"At night, the area was quiet, and it made my loneliness even stronger. I passed a shop that sold cell phones and I knew I had to get one soon to call Felipe. I thought I could ask the Mexican young lady in my house if I could use hers. She seemed friendly. I met her one day. Her name was Viviana, and she had a little girl.

"But I always felt a little worried, and that night after Sea of Cortez when Daisy quickly left, I returned to my place preoccupied about everything. Time weighed on me most of all. I came into the home and set down the chips I brought from Sea of Cortez. Loud music came from the back room where a man stayed. A man who dressed in black, but whom I had never met. I called him El Vampiro because he was always coming in late. We shared a wall in the house, so I heard everything that went on his room.

"After I brushed my teeth and washed my face, I couldn't relax because of his music, but then I heard something else. Another voice in his room, a young woman's, sounded in distress. With my ear to the wall, it sounded like she was struggling. I thought maybe Viviana was in there and that El Vampiro was having his way with her. There was no answer to my knocking at his door. The girl said, "Stop," and so I began banging on the thin wood. Then the girl inside the room screamed. I banged harder and shouted, then pushed my shoulder into the door. It gave to my weight and opened, and there the man stood, naked, stopping me from falling in.

"'What the fuck, old man?' he said.

"Neon purple and the red digital numerals of a bedside clock peeked out from the dark behind the man, along with two timid eyes. The man wasn't as young as I had thought.

"'What do you want?' he said.

"'¿Viviana?' I called into the darkness.

"'You get out of here or I'll have your ass deported. Go on.' He shouted so hard at me I could feel his hot breath on my face.

"The eyes moved from the bed, and their owner shuffled around the room. She came closer to the light in the hallway, terrified. Her eyes thanked me as she slid through the doorway, past the man. It wasn't Viviana, thank God.

"'Hey, come back.' El Vampiro shouted at the girl as he pulled up a pair of shorts.

"The bag on her back was the last I saw of her.

"'What's your name, old man?' El Vampiro said to me. 'Jose? Juan? Huh? Another Mexican, right? You got your papers? Huh?'

"I backed away from his door, toward my bedroom.

"'You better watch out. Do you even understand me? Huh?'

"My hand found the knob of my door. I turned it open, shook my head.

"'Mind your fucking business,' he said, 'or I'm telling Rick and your ass is out of here, you goddamned wetback.'

"I ducked inside my room and closed and locked the door, just as scared as the girl that had escaped. How a man like that lived so closed to me terrified me. José my friend from the Mission had told me about minute men who live near the border, white men who keep their own watch on the area. Maybe that's what El Vampiro was.

"Next morning there were no sounds or sightings of El Vampiro. I thought he at last grew his wings and flew away. I left Viviana a note telling her goodbye and good luck."

"So you got out of there?" Marcos says, "Good idea."

"I could not stay. That was one of my lowest moments. No communication with anyone and nowhere to go. There wasn't much to pack. Only a few pairs of pants, the Sea of Cortez work shirts, socks, underwear. The black athletic shoes— the only pair I had when I came over—were still comfortable. Faith Mission World Center had provided clothes, but they took them all back, along with the shampoos and soaps. Take nothing, they said. Leave everything. It was like I had never even existed there.

"I had bought a chamarra here in San Diego. It was much colder than I expected. The one I bought was in Old Town at a souvenir shop. Black with three skulls on it and "San Diego" written underneath. It reminded me of home, el Dia de los Muertos. How I used to paint my face and visit my dead relatives, offer them food and drinks.

"There was also hope, though it was nothing I could pack. I had to hold it inside me. I couldn't let it die. At that moment, the only thing I knew that made sense was that Joanne was having that reading on Friday and I was going to go to her no matter what. I had to. I couldn't stop. If she remembered me, the universe would have meaning, I thought. There was a God. Even if she didn't remember me—if I had slipped her mind entirely, or if she saw me but rejected me, pretended not to know me, or if she was standing there with her husband or whomever, that would be fine, too. At least I would have the ending I wanted and deserved. I wanted to make what was left of it all on my terms. Then, I could leave this place, walk out the door on my own, with my dignity intact.

"And then I was going to leave back to Mexico once and for all. I wanted to cross on foot and figure out a way to get myself back to Oaxaca. I had done it before when I said goodbye to Joanne in Ensenada. I rode the bus for what seemed like weeks. I returned home and began the new life I knew I had to start without her.

"That day I left my place in San Ysidro, I had to work, and so I made the journey to Sea of Cortez and kept to myself. Daisy wasn't working that morning, so there was no talking, no sharing of my past. All day I thought of the only place I could turn for help, La Bodega López, the only place that felt safe. I would talk to Hugo, the owner to see if he could help me. I needed a place to stay for two more nights. And Hugo López saved me."

"See how lucky you are, Osvaldo," Marcos smiles.

"But I always feel like a sinner."

"But you're surrounded by saints," Marcos says.

"That's what Hugo and his wife Beatriz were to me. That afternoon after work, I stopped in at the Bodega.

"'Osvaldo, compadre?' Hugo greeted me with such care. 'How can we help you today? Shopping?'

"My bag felt heavy then. I'd been thinking about what I could leave behind, whether I should leave it for the next person to move into my room or just put it in the garbage. But that's the problem with memories, you can't get rid of them so easily.

"'My friend, you look troubled.' Hugo approached me. I didn't know this man at all; I had only seen him about four times, and we talked about nothing special each time. Why is it that with strangers, you can tell them everything?

Marcos laughs.

"'I am in trouble,' I said. I don't feel safe in the place where I stay. There's a bad man, a racist. He was raping a girl last night and I stopped him, and then he threatened me. He said he would deport me.'

"'You can stay here with us. You'll be safe here,' Hugo said. 'We've had people here before. In our storeroom we have a bed, and you can bathe in our home.'

"'Oh no, I couldn't. I have to go. Back to Mexico.'

"'You're from Oaxaca, no? How are you going to get back? Do you have any money? We can help you.'

"I wished I had met Hugo when I arrived. Maybe I should have never went to work for the Christian mission. If only I had found Hugo and Beatriz they could have protected me from everything. Adopted me like a stray cat.

"'Just a couple of days. Friday I'm going to see a friend. Then I'm leaving.'

"Hugo set his hand on my shoulder. He brought me toward him, held me next to him like my father once did, before he couldn't. Like Felipe did one last time at the airport.

"'You're safe here,' Hugo said. 'I insist.'

"'Thank you, compadre. I won't bother you and Beatriz.'

"'It's not a bother. You're a human.'

"People like Hugo and his wife are the reason we can go on living with our fellow man and woman, putting faith in them. Trusting them with everything we have.

"That night, the three of us had a quiet dinner in their home. Beatriz had made carne adobada and sopa de arroz. She placed fresh tortillas swaddled in a towel on the table. I waited for them to make their plate first. They had so much together.

"Beatriz kept trying to break the silence asking questions: what's Oaxaca like—she'd never been, how old is Felipe, sorry about my wife.

"Hugo talked over her once, and I could tell that was how their relationship worked—Hugo having to interrupt her to say something, or to make the other person feel more comfortable. They talked to people for a living every day; it made sense they would want to know everything about people and be willing to share about themselves. Teresa and I were somewhat private people. Working at the school we talked to people every day, too, so we needed to enclose ourselves, create some separation from the outside world.

"'You came to work at that religious center, no?' Hugo said.

"Beatriz served more carne adobada. I was full, but I couldn't say no. I reached in for another tortilla anyway.

"'Yes, for the Faith Mission Center and it was a good job. I taught a pottery class.'

"'I heard there were protests there,' Hugo said.

"'Yes, there were. Many people opposed the founder.'

"'Did you meet him?' Beatriz asked.

"'No, only saw him."

"'That's a shame you came all this way for that job,' Beatriz said. 'And now you're at the Sea of Cortez. It's not even real Mexican food.'

"We laughed but it was replaced by silence.

"'Yes, I know. That's why it's time for me to leave. It's hard to make a life here. My family is still in Oaxaca. I miss my son, my grandson, but it was my dream to come here one day.'

"'It's a nice place. We've had a good life here," Hugo said. "Our sons were born here. They've grown up to be good men. We sometimes talk about going back to Mexico to retire.'

"'That sounds nice. You two have each other.'

"Hugo changed the subject sensing my loneliness. 'You mentioned a friend you need to see,' Hugo said.

"'Yes, she's—'

"'Ay! Get on with it. Tell us.' Beatriz lit up.

"'Bea,' Hugo touched her forearm.

"'He's in love,' she said.

"'It's been so long, thirty years. I don't know if she'll remember me.'

"'Who is she?' Beatriz asked.

"'She's a writer, an author.'

"'Ay! How nice!' she said.

"'Joanne Watson. Do you know of her?'

"'Gringa?' Beatriz seemed disappointed.

"'Bea, it's none of our business.' Hugo stood, began clearing the plates.

"'Yes, we met a long time ago in Oaxaca. She has a reading soon. On Friday. That's where I'm trying to go. I need to find where it will be.'

"Beatriz stood, face bright. 'You two put the dishes in the washer. I'm going to get my computer. We're going to find this Joanne for Osvaldo.'

"And so there she was again, what Daisy had begun to tell me. Joanne was reading from her book Friday in La Jolla at a store called Warwick's. Beatriz was beaming with excitement.

"'Very pretty lady,' Beatriz said. 'Look, her book is called *Slip Soul*. We can take you.'

"'Yes, let us drive you,' Hugo said.

"'No, I'm fine. I'll take the trolley.' My heart was racing. The title. It was the same as my old copy.

"'But it doesn't go all the way to this part of La Jolla,' Beatriz said. 'We have to take you; you don't even have a phone.'

"'Better to be safe with us,' Hugo said.

"'That's fine, thank you. But tomorrow, I'm taking the trolley to work.'

"'Hugo, mi amor, show Osvaldo to the room," Beatriz typed into the computer.

"From their kitchen, Hugo led me out a side door that went directly to their storeroom.

"'On that other side is the store.' He pointed to another door on far side of the room. 'I keep that door locked, so there's nothing to worry about. And you can come through this door anytime you want.'

"The corner Los López had arranged into a tiny residence felt more like a home than anything I'd experienced in a long time. The bed had a second mattress underneath that rolled out, and there were several pillows and blankets, along with a smaller mattress, as though for a crib. The dresser, similar to the chest at my last place, was full of clothes for men, women, and children. T-shirts, socks, underwear, sweatshirts. In the bottom drawer, shoes. The two floor lamps made the place feel warm, like a hotel room, and all of it was arranged near a narrow door, where inside there was a sink, mirror, and toilet.

"'This is perfect, thank you again.'

"'We just had a man and his two older children stay here. They were on their way to Oakland. Do you know where that is? Anyway, it doesn't matter. His wife is coming up later, but they have a little girl, a toddler, and they were scared to come. They're taking babies at the border, sending them away from their mothers.'

"'Where do they go?'

"'Detention centers, I guess. Nobody knows.'

"'How can she come?'

"'Maybe they go through New Mexico. The man said he was going to save up for a flight for them. He even said maybe they'll go to Canada. You see, they were from Guatemala. They can't find work. They feel unsafe.'

"'And here I am, trying to find a woman. I'm so selfish.'

"'Quit beating yourself up, my friend. Make yourself at home and don't worry about anything else but you tonight. And in the morning, I'm going to give you a phone. You need a phone, Osvaldo.'

"'You are too kind,' I said.

"We shook hands and Hugo left for the evening.

"Under the woody smell of colorful cardboard, plastic bags, green bananas and oranges, I felt comforted. My bag and all it had inside of it was nothing compared to what Hugo and Beatriz had spent their lives building, how they were able to give so much to other people. I took my black shoes off and put them under the bed. The shelves toward the foot of the bed held glass candles with Jesus showing his burning sacred heart, Our Lady of Guadalupe eyes cast down on Juan Diego adoring her. Next to them were packages of incense and cans of miracle spray to ward off bad spirits. There was an assortment of packaged crucifixes and rosaries. It was possible Hugo and Beatriz placed this shelf here to soothe their guests in transit. This makeshift altar a place to leave their worries and sins before the next move. That night was my best sleep in the United States."

"YOUR STORIES, OSVALDO," Marcos says. "Some people tell lies, or make things up to sound better, but you, tío, these are incredible."

"That's all life is. Stories. You must be hungry. When they bring dinner, you have to eat."

Marcos laughs. "I think that was lunch and dinner."

"It was terrible." I close the pages, about to stuff them back in the envelope.

"How much more can you read today?" Marcos says.

"For you, carnal, I'll keep reading. But I'm going to need to rest soon."

Slip Soul by Joe DeVries
Chapter 6

Nine months later

August that year turned to a dry September with no more storms, and behind it came a calm and quiet winter in Zicatela. The usual South American tourists checked in at the Bungalows, then checked out, Oaxaquñeos came for Christmas and New Year's, and before long, it was spring, and then la Semana Santa, when more Mexicanos checked in. Pablo loved these times with his people, as much as the other seasons, when foreign visitors came and went.

Of these, Ruggy, Jucélia, and Renata indeed stayed. They kept their room at the Bungalows for a month, one of the longest terms Pablo had seen, and then they moved to Casa Medrano. Pablo had found them the place by asking his friend Héctor Medrando who owned the apartments if his friends could move in. Medrano's place was walking distance to the Bungalows, which helped the girls who had begun working with Pablo. They cleaned rooms and helped on the patio during breakfast and happy hours. Ruggy kept his close eye, of course, but he was busy with his own projects. With Pablo's help, Ruggy's plans to open a beach bar were coming to life. He wanted to call it Paradiso.

In those months, one scene repeated itself: on the nights Pablo played at La Sirena, the group sat either on the beach to keep the party going or went back to Pablo's apartment in the motel if the weather was cool. In either place, they kept the drinks flowing, the joints passing, all with Pablo strumming in the background. Cousin Jorge always invited another girl or two to introduce to his single cousin, but Jorge ended up dancing with all of them, including Renata. In between his songs, Pablo and Ruggy built their friendship, with Ruggy doing most of the building of himself up around Pablo by sharing stories of his time in the ring. And when he wasn't enveloping Jucélia, Ruggy continued to sell Pablo on his idea for the bar.

"It will be the ultimate," Ruggy was always saying.

Lo ultimo qué? Pablo thought.

Ruggy's attempt at Spanish with a trace of Portuguese didn't translate.

"English," Pablo had said. "I'm learning, too."

"Like the pinnacle. The absolute best," Ruggy said.

"Lo mejor," Pablo said.

"We'll have a Wunderbar," Ruggy said.

"What's a wonder bar?" Pablo said.

"It's a machine that pours all the drinks from one tube."

"Can't we just pour them?" Pablo said.

This conversation grew and with it more plans. Surfboards for the bar tops. Old stools from a closed down restaurant Pablo knew about. Palm fronds from that dying tree south of town they could use for the palapa. Ruggy kept Pablo part of the plan and Pablo supported it, he wanted to see his friend succeed. But Pablo couldn't deny the unspoken clues Jucélia kept leaving. When they all sat on the beach or in Pablo's place and Ruggy would speak of his imaginary bar, elbowing Jucélia to gain her support, she only nodded, sometimes smiled to appease him.

"Won't it be great, babe?" Ruggy said. "We can have you and Nata dance for Carnaval."

Once, Jucélia simply moved away to be with her sister who was dancing with Jorge and another girl. Her silent communication with Pablo carried over into their work, and Pablo let it. His feelings for her had grown strong inside of him, too. If Ruggy wasn't already up after his morning run and lingering around the patio, Pablo and Jucélia shared a newfound companionship setting out the juice and coffee, wiping tables, Pablo frying eggs, and Jucélia serving. This quiet friendship was one in which they only had to be around each other to feel comfort. They laughed, teased each other, brushed up against one another, sometimes by chance, others on purpose.

One time, with his hands full, he called her back to the cooking station, asking for her to get more oil.

"It's under here," he said, pointing to the small door at his feet. She brought the new bottle of canola up to him and a strand of Pablo's hair, always pulled back with a tie had come undone and was hanging alongside his cheekbone. With no prompting at all, Jucélia grabbed it and tucked it behind his ear.

"Thank you," he said, staring into her eyes, she returning his gaze. The cool tension that had been building for months increased to a simmer in that moment, until it was broken by the sound of a bucket hitting the tiled floor of the patio. Just a few feet away, Renata stood with her cleaning supplies wearing a sly smile. She picked up what she had dropped and said, "I knew it."

Jucélia flushed and backed away from Pablo.

"Knew what?" Pablo said.

"I know my sister," Renata said.

"Nata, please."

Just then, another voice. Ruggy.

"'Nata, please' what?" he seemed to appear out of nowhere, but he was back from his run, shirtless and sweating.

"Oh, nothing," Jucélia said, pointing out onto the patio. "I was asking her to take a coffee over to that table."

Pablo watched the sisters share a secret glance. He understood they had their own private language.

"Coffee sounds great. I'll take a cup." Ruggy said. "Hey, Pablo. Will you help me move some palm fronds today? I found more far down the *malecón*. Can we use your Bronco?"

"Yes, yes, that's fine," Pablo said.

"And it's okay if we keep them in your shed? Right?"

Ruggy's dream was coming to life with all the items and equipment he'd collected and since stored in the shed behind Los Bungalows—the shed meant for Pablo's tools and storage for the motel.

"Yes, yes, Ruggy," Pablo said. "After I'm finished here, and after I do some work in one of the rooms."

"Is this all for now?" Jucélia asked Pablo.

"Yes, it's slow now," Pablo said.

"Well, I'm going home to take a shower and rest," Jucélia said.

"I'll go with you," Renata said.

"Hey," Ruggy called to Jucélia. "That coffee?"

Jucélia turned back, went to the coffee station and filled a cup. She handed it to Ruggy, and Pablo saw another secret language, one of punisher and punished.

Later that night, as Pablo turned off his light to go to sleep, he could not rest. He twisted in every direction trying to find a comfortable position, but nothing worked. He went to his small kitchen to make the tea Tía Claudia had given to help him fall asleep. The nights he drank that, he almost always had a journey outside of himself, and he often wondered if Claudia had put something in it. Her remedies and potions were limitless.

A few sips and relaxation arrived at last. It wasn't the loneliness that bothered him—he had learned to live with that since he was a young boy. It was that he knew where he should be, whom he should be with. He couldn't remember a time when he had been as lovesick as now.

Back in his bed, eyes closed and breathing slow, Pablo idled in the tiny passageway between this side and that. The feeling radiated first in his toes as the tingle of a deadened sleeping limb times a thousand, accompanied by a buzz louder than a million bees. The electricity penetrated his ankles, then coursed up his shins and knees, crept into his loins, then into his stomach, chest and head, every inch of his body succumbing to a gripping paralysis.

The bed swallowed him downward, his body sinking into the fibers, then the sudden separation overcame him—an unhinging of flesh and spirit.

A forceful upward tug extracted him from the quicksand of his bed, though it wasn't his physical body that lifted. Separating from his organs and bones was his very being, a translucent and airy form that was all of Pablo's vital energy, released from its human shell. Below his vaporous shape, his body lay, still sleeping.

He never used this power to spy on people. It would be an invasion of their privacy, and against his own beliefs. But tonight, he needed to see her. He wanted to check in on her.

Pablo floated above Casa Medrando in the still night, his airy form moving toward door number eight. He appeared before the door, and without needing to touch it, he passed through the wood as a living ghost, his shape still the form of a man.

He hadn't been in their place in a while, and remembered it being bare: a mattress, a lone chair, a trunk. But that was almost a year ago. They had since settled in, Ruggy especially. Posters with Ruggy and his opponents' masked faces, time stamped with the arenas and dates, covered two walls. On another, columns of flattened masks and ball caps flanked two large boards of Polaroids, autographed pictures, magazine pages, and ticket stubs. In the corner sat a weight bench and dumbbells with a large mirror. Ruggy knew how to find what he wanted.

Pablo moved only a few feet before he saw her. With her legs tucked underneath her, Jucélia sat at the end of an old sofa with a pen in her hand resting on top of the pages of her diary. A candle burned on the small table beside her. She wrote some, then stopped to wipe her eyes. Pablo moved closer to her, feeling both her pain and her warmth. Once, she set her pen down on the pages and held her left wrist with her writing hand, nursing it, holding it close to her heart.

Slip Soul by Joe DeVries
Chapter 7

29 Maio 1979

It's like I can feel you with me now, Pablo. Like you are right here next to me. Oh, how I need you now, like I needed you today. After Renata caught me touching your hair, she knew. She teased me in private and I begged her not to say anything, she promised, but it didn't matter because Lester already knew something was going on. He's perceptive like that. He might have been watching all the while. I was playing that over in my head all day, which is why I thought he treated me the way he did afterward.

After work, I went back home to take a shower and rest and he arrived just after Renata and I had spoken. He cornered me and said he wanted to make love, but I wasn't in the mood. Then he said it was because I was thinking of you. I suppose that is correct. I lost my feelings for Lester a long time ago. I don't have passion for him. Not for what he does to me.

Then he grabbed my wrist, held and squeezed it until I caved to his strength. Then he—I can't even write it here. And how Renata stays in her room. I know she knows what goes on, but she just looks the other way. I'm so alone here, and I'm so scared.

Slip Soul by Joe DeVries
Chapter 8

Summer had arrived with its heat, and so had Ruggy's urgency to complete Paradiso.

"We'll be open in a few weeks," Ruggy said. "Maybe less. I wish we had made it the Fourth of July weekend. Independence Day would have been perfect."

"For you," Jorge smiled. "Not for us."

With longer days, the men had begun working into the evening, building, and setting up the structure. They had erected the four beams to hold up the pitched palapa roof and constructed the bar with the surfboard tops. On slower days at the Bungalows, Ruggy had the girls help by weaving the leaves together to go onto the roof.

One afternoon, when the whole group was working, Jorge kept trying to make eye contact with his cousin, winking at Pablo. Pablo stopped to acknowledge him, and Jorge made eyes at Jucélia, smiling and hinting.

"I have to run to the shed," Pablo said. "I'll bring back drinks. Come with me, Jorge."

"I'll come," Renata said.

"No, we've got it," Pablo said.

The cousins headed back toward the shed, Jorge already whispering.

"What do you have, *primo*?" Pablo asked.

Far enough from the group, Jorge let it out.

"I heard Jucélia likes you."

"What? No. Who said that?"

Pablo's denial fell flat with Jorge.

"Come on, *primo*, who do you think? Renata. She told me."

"Your girlfriend, no?" Pablo teased him back.

"Friend. With benefits."

"How do you do that, man? Don't mess around like that."

"Stop it. You're not a saint." Jorge hit Pablo's arm. "But anyway, she said Jucélia goes around thinking about you all time. She doesn't even like Ruggy. Imagine, primo, you and Jucélia? She's beautiful."

Jorge paused. The brief silence between them was a confirmation of the idea—of the reality—Jorge described. It would be beautiful. It would be a dream for him to be with her.

"But, man," Jorge said, "Ruggy would kill you."

Another moment of quiet truth.

"That's why I'm not doing anything," Pablo said.

"So, you like her, too?" Jorge said.

"I didn't say that."

"Come on, you like her." Jorge elbowed him. "You like her. Look at you."

Pablo showed nothing to his cousin. If Jorge and Renata were gossiping like this, even a drop of information had the potential to become an ocean of trouble.

"She's a nice girl and I want her to be happy."

"Nice girl?" Jorge said. "You shut up. If you want her to be happy, you need to send that gringo home."

Jorge's words hit harder than anything he'd been thinking about lately, even his feelings for Jucélia. He could fantasize all day and visit her on his night journeys, but there was still something blocking the way. There would always be a suppression of what both of them wanted, and only one thing would cure it: the absence of Ruggy.

"Well, everyone knows she's unhappy," Pablo said. "I feel bad for her."

"Renata says he beats her."

"He's ... I can see that he's bad," Pablo said.

The two arrived at the shed. They had nothing to retrieve, needing only a place to speak in private.

"I wonder, *primo*, why are we going around making him happy anyway? Making his dreams come true?"

"Because he's always had it that way," Pablo said. "Let's take some drinks back to them and then end it for the day over there. I need to finish some work here and practice for tonight at La Sirena."

Between his songs at La Sirena, the group took tequila shots and ate chicharrones, laughed and smiled. Ruggy was in a festive mood, putting his big arms around people, telling them about Paradiso. "Right there on the beach," he pointed.

Orly Galván, owner of La Sirena, had come up to Pablo to talk about the new place.

"And you're behind this?" he said. "Are you going to run me out of business?"

"No, no, they're two different places. Just let him have his time," Pablo said.

"I give it two months," Orly said. "After the summer, when all the tourists have gone home, I'd say it goes under. And look where it's at. Not the safest place for a business. We're due for some more hurricanes."

Pablo nodded and shrugged, but inside he agreed, and he felt a little sorry for himself. He was sorry for letting himself be used, because that's what was going on, and he at last acknowledged it. Sure, he was fascinated that a luchador—even a gringo one—happened to come to town and settle in, thinking they would be friends. And they were, but it had become clear it was for a reason. Ruggy wasn't a man who helped others. He was a man who helped himself.

Just before Pablo went back on to the small stage, Ruggy sidled up to him and draped his arm around Pablo.

"Pablo," he said. "You've helped me so much here. You know everybody and they all love you. You're everyone's best friend. You're my only real friend here. You know that? Do you know that?"

"I'm happy for you, man," Pablo said, smelling the alcohol on Ruggy's breath.

"You're the best, man," Ruggy said. "You're my best man. Hey, do you want to be my best man? Shhh ... don't say anything, but I'm going to ask Jucélia to marry me."

"I have to get up on stage, man." Pablo pointed and moved away from Ruggy's grip. "Married?" Pablo mouthed the word as he walked away from Ruggy.

Ruggy nodded and shouted at Pablo as he walked up, "Wooo!" Ruggy said. "Go, Pablo! Wooo!"

On stage, Ruggy ran his pick over the strings. He drew blank for a moment and had forgotten what he was going to sing. Gazing into the crowd, the faces of everyone he knew and loved stared back up at him, waiting for him to make his move. He looked only at one person, and though she tried to hide her eyes, she focused on him too as he began to play.

Slip Soul by Joe DeVries
Chapter 9

18 Julho 1979

I am surrounded by alcohol. In this place, there are cases of beer, bottles of tequila, mezcal, rum, cases of wine, vodka and mixers. Lester worships them. He counts them and writes them down in a book he has. I dislike all of this around me, but I own it. He's used some of my earnings from the Bungalows to buy this. He has his own money, but he's used so much of it already. He just needs to get his own job. He thinks he's going to become a rich man as a bartender. I wonder if he will make the money back or drink them himself.

And now he talks about getting married. Now, after all this time, he wants to settle down with me. What have I been for him up until now? His toy? A doll? A whore? Something he uses and beats up and leaves in the gutter.

In the early days, when he was starting to train at the fighting clubs and trying to make a name for himself, we started to see each other. He was sweet then, but it didn't last. He started to work security at a discoteca but started more fights than he stopped. He quickly hurt his reputation, and no one wanted to work with him, saying he was too aggressive. He saw me trying to better myself as I was taking classes, and that threatened him. That's when

124

the comments began. They were small. About where I lived, the food I ate and what I wore. I put up with it because I thought it was love. It wasn't. It was his control over me. As he trained more, he became more aggressive. The more aggressive, the more his insults and mind games. Renata told me to leave him, and I tried, but then he began his threats and then he started to get physical.

And then he wanted to move to Mexico. To run away again from his problems. He wanted to get into the lucha scene here. I should have said no, just stayed instead of following along with him. Even though I followed him, and because he made me follow him, I'm happy I came because I found you, Pablo. This was what it was all for. Coming here to this place was meant for me. You are who I imagine when I think of marrying someone. You are the person I want to be with. Not Lester.

I told him he has to ask my father first. Lester never met my father. I hardly see my father anyway, and it really does not matter. I just said that to stall him. I don't want to marry him. He's forcing it on me like everything else. I don't even want to be with him now.

My fantasy is to have this place all to ourselves. It is paradise, and you make it so. I dream of waking up with you every day, the warmth of the sun pouring in, the sound of the waves bringing us to life, our bodies next to each other, protecting one another.

But it can't be this way. Not now. Maybe not ever. Maybe I should just run away myself and then tell you where I am later so you can find me.

THE ONLY WAY WE KNOW that it's nighttime is when Nurse Vargas comes in to check on us. My throat is sore from talking and reading all day and I ask for something hot to drink. She says she'll try to get something. They're always saying that here.

"You two are going back into the detention center tomorrow before the lunch hour. You can come back here for pain medication when you need it," she says.

"What if he can't walk?" Marcos asks.

"We'll decide what to do, but for now, those are the rules. I don't want to see you go back out there either, but I have to follow orders. Another round of these pills and you will sleep solid, and we'll check you in the morning."

She peeks at the stack of papers. "Is that what came for you earlier?"

"It's a love letter," Marcos says.

"Well, whoever it is must really love you." She hands each of us two large pills.

Marcos is out before I can count to ten. I lay there in the room, now dim. After some time, Nurse Vargas comes back with a Styrofoam cup with a tea bag and hands it to me.

"It's chamomile from me. You need your rest."

I sip the tea and set aside *Slip Soul* for the night.

11 - OTAY MESA BREAKFAST

THE NEXT MORNING, WE WAKE TO THE bright lights of the clinic coming to life. After breakfast of applesauce and a sweet roll, Marcos wants to return to Puerto Escondido. Before I read, he's curious about *the gift*.

"And the out of body travel, is that something you didn't tell me about, tío? If you can do that, why not just fly out of here?" Marcos says.

We laugh, how nice that would be.

"It has happened to me before. And If I could control it, I would get out of here. Leave my dead body right here."

"Did you tell her about it?" Marcos says.

"I think I mentioned it once. I know we talked about it after the mushrooms with my Tía Claudia. I think her mind was opened after that."

"But I see how she took your story. You don't feel used?" Marcos asks.

"I feel alive more than anything. I am here, in her pages."

"Read more, please. And then, you have to tell me about when you finally met her here in the United States. I still don't know that."

I have been avoiding that story. It's too difficult to talk about, but I know that I can share it with Marcos. I've told him everything else, and I trust him with my life.

I pull the stack of papers out again and we return to the beach.

With only a couple of days left before the opening of Paradiso, Pablo was distracted by his thoughts of Jucélia and the silent affair they had been having. After he had played and sang that night at La Sirena, sending his words to her, he traveled out of his body and went to visit her. He wanted to lift her away as though he was an angel able to take them to the real paradise.

He'd often wondered if his power was what it meant to be an angel, but that thought was met with the reality that it should not be that lonely. In the days when his mother had passed away, Pablo could not understand when the priest delivering Eva's last rites had said, "Forever and ever." What would you do, Pablo thought, with all that time all alone? Who would you be with?

Tonight, he decided not to go visit Jucélia because seeing her there, either sleeping uncomfortably next to Ruggy, writing in her diary wiping her tears, or worse, Ruggy violating her, would only infuriate him, and what could he do anyway as an invisible spirit?

He lay alone in his bed trying to relax himself, telling himself not to travel. When he at last found sleep deep into the night, he felt the sensations again, though this time, the release began in his toes—the tingling there a tease of the forceful jerking that followed as the life in his legs, waist, then torso, drained out of his sleeping body. His arms, neck, and head were the last to separate from himself, lifting like the clumsy, dancing *marionetas* the *vendedores* sold in town at the tourist shops.

With only the last few fibers of his soul still attached to his human head, his two forms all but unhinged from one another, Pablo fought back, willing his spirit to return. Something about this departure did not feel right. As the vibrations steeped, he gave into the energy and crossed over.

He flung up and out of his home above the Bungalows, hurling skyward into the canopy of night, a deep blue canvas splattered with stars so close, he tried to reach up and take one. As fast as he had shot into the heavens, he plummeted backward, caving toward earth. He grabbed in all directions to slow his fall, then slammed to a stop, as though strung up, hovering face first over a pitch-black chasm. The suspension holding him up snapped, and he tumbled headlong into the pit, the mouth of whatever it was now swallowing him whole.

On his descent, the outline of a face pulsed from the darkness, growing bigger and clearer, replicating with each beat. An enormous head covered in stitched green and yellow fabric surrounded Pablo in the vacuum. The head turned and Ruggy's face appeared, sneering, gnashing his exposed teeth, roaring over the rising din of an invisible audience hissing and booing. The cries and chants of thousands of fans rose to hysteria. They booed in unison.

Pablo slammed back-first onto a cold, hard mat. He was in the wrestling ring.

DING! The bell.

Ruggy, in full costume, bright green pants with yellow lightning bolts on the sides of his legs, gold boots, no shirt, and his wild eyes, flickering from the diamond-holes in his mask, staggered out from a dark corner grunting with his arms swinging.

"Boo! Boo! Boo!" The audience screamed.

Pablo scrambled to his feet and threw jabs. He knew to aim for the gut if he couldn't land one on Ruggy's face. The man was a foot taller, so a solid uppercut would do it. Pablo took his stance and braced himself.

The crowd went wild. The mat shook, almost bounced Pablo off of it. Ruggy pressed forward, but it wasn't his feet that were shaking the mat. Pablo turned back. Behind him, an even bigger man loomed above them. He stood in blue pants and a glittery mask, shiny white slivers for eyeholes. The crowd chanted, "Salva-dor, Salva-dor, Salva-dor!" Their savior was here.

Pablo shot up over the ring as El Salvador lunged for Ruggy and lifted him up like a toy. He spun Ruggy around and threw him down to the mat. Ruggy leapt to his feet, and El Salvador aimed his head into Ruggy's stomach, slamming him against the rope. Ruggy sailed into El Salvador's outstretched arm, stopping him cold, sending him to the mat. The crowd screamed, "Salva-dor, Salva-dor, Salva-dor!"

El Salvador knelt down next to Ruggy, flipped him over, and locked Ruggy's head into his python arms. El Salvador lifted The Rugger's head up and back to show the crowd.

The invisible audience, now popping with the light of a million cameras in the pitch black, chanted again—first a whisper—then wild screams, over and over in perfect unison: ¡Desenmascarar! ¡Desenmascarar! Unmask him, unmask him.

Pablo, who had been viewing this from above was now back on the mat and viewing this scene as though he was enacting it. He held his hands up to look at them and caught a glimpse of himself—he appeared to be dressed as a luchador himself, as though he had embodied El Salvador.

The audience screamed again, yelling to unmask The Rugger. Pablo, in the form of El Salvador, slapped his palm down onto Ruggy's crown and began to pull the mask back. Ruggy fought it with all his might. He kicked the canvas, flailed his arms to grab Pablo.

Pablo flung Ruggy's mask off, letting it fly like a dirty sock. Ruggy submitted and dropped his sweaty head to the mat. Pablo stood and stretched out his arms into a "T," the same victory move of El Salvador.

Defeated, Ruggy turned over, eyes laser-focused upward into the darkness behind Pablo. The crowd screamed louder, issuing more boos and wicked chants. His eyes grew wider until the whites expanded, and Pablo felt himself falling downward to the glaring light.

With this, Pablo recoiled back into himself—this journey not a journey, but a nightmare. He sat up in his bed panting and grabbed his watch on the nightstand. No telling how long he'd been asleep. His watch read five in the morning. It was time to wake up and get to work. He reached again to the stand to make sure his master keys were there. They clicked in his grip and simply touching them calmed him. They were his security.

Later that morning, Pablo tried to focus on his work, quickly setting the morning provisions out, turning the music up higher than usual. No guests were up yet, however Jucélia arrived soon after. Across the patio from each other, anticipating in the silence they had grown used to, they moved toward each other by instinct.

"Jucélia," he offered his hand, knowing all she was going through. "I'm worried."

She took his hand and squeezed it, and this triggered both of them to grasp at each other, awkward at first, his hand tugging at the bottom of her blouse, she trying to grip his waist. Though the quiet morning offered some privacy, they knew they should not be seen so close together.

"Here," he said, "follow me."

Pablo led her to the lobby, which was still dim with the curtains closed. Once inside, he acted on what he knew was coming. Taking her in his arms, he embraced her for the first time, and she returned his hug, the two of them pressing into each other in an act they had suppressed for too long.

"I've needed you," she said.

"I know, I want to help you," he said, then with their faces only inches apart, their lips met and so began a gentle but urgent kiss, both clutching to each other trying to catch their breath.

"No," she said, "Stop, this is—we could get caught."

She looked all around, nervous and starting to tremble.

"Don't worry, you're safe, you're safe," he assured her, but she was uncomfortable, trying to turn to leave.

"Here," she said reaching into her pocket, handing Pablo a piece of folded paper. "Read this later when no one's watching."

And with that, she slipped out of the lobby. For a moment he thought she had vanished, but then he saw her back on the patio, wrapping an apron around her waist, serving a cup of coffee to the first guest. He hid the note in the pocket of his shorts and walked toward the patio, then was stopped by footsteps and a voice behind him.

"Pab." It was Ruggy, always up early. "Ready to finish moving everything in?"

Ruggy had called that Friday "Move In" day, the day they would carry everything that was left in the shed out to the beach bar. The plan was to open the next evening. Ruggy's excitement was peaking. He had tacked red flyers on street posts and boards and had littered them around the Bungalows.

"I made more flyers," he said. "I'm going to leave them on the tables here in the patio."

"That's fine," Pablo said.

"You tired this morning?" Ruggy asked.

"Yes, I had a strange dream last night," Pablo said. "About you."

"You dreaming about me?" Ruggy said. "I'm flattered."

"I dreamed about you in the ring."

Ruggy stopped, turned to Pablo and crunched up his eyebrows. "Oh?" he said.

"It was nothing, just as if I was watching a match."

"Oh. Okay. I've been having strange dreams, too," Ruggy said. "Maybe it's living next to the ocean. Hey, we're going to party at your place tonight, right?"

"Yeah, tonight. My place," Pablo said. "Go get some coffee. Jucélia's out on the patio."

"I know. She was up early."

Ruggy paused, looked into Pablo instead of at him. Pablo returned nothing but thought of the note in his pocket.

"Women, you know?" Ruggy said. "Can't live with them, can't live—" Ruggy waited for Pablo to finish the phrase. "Can't live without them ... you never heard that?"

"It's true," Pablo said. "You can't live without them. Look, I have to work in the lobby for a while. You want to move everything later this afternoon?"

Pablo turned to go back into the lobby, but Ruggy stopped him again.

"Oh, I can start now. I'll take the keys now."

"I need them now," Pablo said, patting his other pocket, his master keys jingling inside. "Go sit on the patio, and I'll see you in a little while."

Ruggy shrugged, stepped back.

"See you then," he said.

The note seemed to pulse in Pablo's pocket, its words already speaking to him as he retreated back into the lobby, behind the front desk, and into the door that led to his apartment. He pulled it out, his hands nervous and urgent, unfolding it, her written words calling to him.

Pablo,

I come to you in confidence. Please do not show this to anyone, and please, if you can, help me. I fear for my life with Lester. He watches my every move. His behavior is at the point of madness. He says he's going to marry me, and this upsets me more than anything. I do not want to be with him. I've lost whatever it was I had for him a long time ago.

But I must also tell you the feelings I have for you. I've never believed in love at first sight, but when I

*met you, I felt something magical, and now I want to be
more than a friend with you, Pablo. I am sorry if this
is too much for you, but I believe you feel this too.*

*What scares me is that Lester suspects all of this.
He knows already that I have pulled away, and he's jealous
of you. Not only for what you have, but that I may have
your attention. He's using you to open this bar, and so
I fear for you, too.*

Pablo, what can I do? What can we do? Please help.

Beijos,

Cici

Pablo's heart pounded. He knew this was coming and he
had to do something to save her, to save them. His first
thought: Tía Claudia. He took a pen and paper and wrote
down instructions for Jucélia should anything happen. He
wrote which roads to take, which landmarks to look for,
which house to find near the Rio Virgen in El Camarón up
in the hills. *Six miles east out of town. Tell my Tía
Claudia I sent you. She will trust you because you know
me. Pat the top of your head and say abrazo. It was our
way of saying we need help. You can take my car. There's
a spare set of keys in the glove compartment in a tin
case. Once you're there, wait for me. I will come for
you. I will protect you.*

That afternoon, the men pulled the stools and
glassware and plates, bar cloths, and jars of cherries
and olives and mixers and ice chests out to Paradiso.
They stepped back and Ruggy crossed his arms, looking
with pride at what would soon come to life. The women had
joined them there on the beach at sundown. Watching the
waves crash with the sun hovering above the horizon, an
unusual fog rolled in cooling the beach, sending them
inside. Pablo looked back at the ocean, knowing something
was about to change. With Ruggy still distracted by his

creation, Pablo was able to move toward Jucélia and hand her his note. She grabbed it and tucked it away into her waistband, but not without Renata and Jorge catching a glimpse of this, then sharing their own secret smile.

Slip Soul by Joe DeVries
Chapter 11

As the meeting place for the group, Pablo's apartment had a vibe of comfort and security for the friends. Tonight however, with a Bob Marley record playing, the mood was subdued, and despite his efforts to liven everyone up, Jorge the jokester couldn't seem to get anyone to laugh, especially with Renata and Jucélia who stood in the kitchen most of the time, Renata stationing herself in the side doorway that opened to the outside so she could smoke.

The men passed a joint and a bottle of mezcal, but the beer they had open in front of them on the coffee table sat ignored, sweating away its coldness.

"Nervous about tomorrow?" Jorge said to Ruggy. "Don't worry. People will come. Mexicans are curious."

"No, I'm not nervous." Ruggy stood up and began to pace. "I'm just a little pissed off."

"Why?" Jorge said.

Ruggy pointed toward the wall that separated the living space from the kitchen. "That," he said.

"The wall?" Jorge said.

Pablo, who had been strumming his guitar, stopped playing.

"No, her." Ruggy stopped pacing.

"Women trouble," Jorge said.

"She's been acting like this for a while," Ruggy turned to Pablo. "And I know why. Jucélia. Get in here."

"I think we're going to go home," Renata called back at the men.

"No, you're not," Ruggy said, walking toward them.

The girls came to the living area but kept their distance. Jucélia held Renata's hand.

"I know what's going on here," Ruggy moved on Jucélia. "Are you screwing this guy?" He pointed back to Pablo, who had stood, pushing his guitar to the floor.

"Ruggy, what are you talking about?" Pablo said.

"Don't deny it, I see how you look at her. And you, writing in your diary. I know what you wrote in there. I read it. You love him. All I've done for you, and this is how you treat me? Is this how you treat me?"

Ruggy grabbed Jucélia's arm and Renata held the other, trying to move her sister away. Pablo and Jorge went for Ruggy to pull him away, but he was immovable.

"Get off of me," he said, turning around with the evil sneer Pablo had seen in his dream. Ruggy dropped his grip on Jucélia for a moment to confront the men. Pablo locked his eyes on Jucélia and patted his head, their symbol for her to leave.

"Go," he whispered.

Ruggy saw this and flung around to stop Jucélia who had grabbed Renata's arm to take her with her. Jucélia urged them along crying for Ruggy to stop. He got his hands on Renata as the girls had almost made it out of the side door.

"You get back here!" Ruggy screamed, his grip now firmly on Renata. Jorge kept at him as Pablo went for Jucélia, but he was met by Ruggy's leg, which he had stuck out to trip him. Jucélia stood in the doorway unattached. From the floor, Pablo said it again, this time louder. "Go. Run."

Jucélia turned to her sister in Ruggy's grip and cried for her, however the show was already in play, and Ruggy was at the center of the ring. He had one arm on Renata, his other swatting at Jorge, and he had since moved his foot over Pablo's back pinning him to the ground. In tears, Jucélia fled.

What happened next was a blur of jabs, kicks, and leaps as Pablo had broken free. It was a *lucha libre* in miniature with two David's attacking one Goliath who held his victim, also delivering her own hits on the monster. Ruggy appeared to waver between rage and enjoyment knowing he had the upper hand, shouting the truth he'd held back at them as if the blows and kicks were not enough.

"You're not man enough for her," he spat at Pablo. "You're dumb. And easy to control."

Ruggy kept a lock on Pablo as Pablo continued to kick and punch where he could. He at last drove an elbow into Ruggy's stomach, which knocked the air from him and sent him backward. While this was a small win, the war continued, and that blurry scene, ridiculous in nature of men trying to prove themselves came to an end in pitch black as Pablo sustained a hit to the head sending him straight to the carpet in the living room of his apartment.

Slip Soul by Joe DeVries
Chapter 12

In the hour before dawn, while the sky was purple with fading stars and a vanishing moon, Pablo's spirit had been in flight heading toward El Camarón. After Ruggy had knocked him to the floor, he fell into a blackout sleep and had stayed there as the rest of the night moved on. Over the hillsides and river, Pablo's spirit dove to Claudia's home where he had sent Jucélia. Once inside of Claudia's home, he found it still and quiet with the ticking clock in her kitchen the only sound.

Pablo's airy body went to the sitting room first where he found candles still burning as sunlight started to permeate through the dark blue curtains. On one of the sofas, Jucélia was tucked in a blanket, deep in sleep. She had arrived safely, and she looked the most peaceful he had seen her since she had come to Zicatela. The candles, a burnt stick of incense, and rosary beads nearby told Pablo that Claudia may have given Jucélia a healing, perhaps praying with her or over her through the night.

The seeping morning light began to dim, and in his astral form, Pablo felt the tug on his earthly body that this journey was ending. The tugging grew urgent followed by the electric sensations of his spirit re-entering his flesh, all with a voice increasing in volume and concern.

"¡Pablo! ¡Despíertate!" The voice shouted. A man's voice. Jorge.

Pablo, now back in one piece on the shag carpet, awoke to his cousin shaking his shoulders.

"Pablito, I thought you were dead. You looked like a corpse." Jorge helped him sit up.

"She's safe." Pablo blinked and ran his hands through his hair.

"Jucélia?" Jorge said. "No man, she ran away. She's gone."

"But she's in El Camaron with Claudia. I saw her."

"Are you having those weird dreams again?" Jorge said.

Pablo stood and tried to shake himself back to reality. His head ached and his mouth had the taste and texture of dry sand. The record player still spun with the needle skipping off the turntable.

"How long have I been here?" Pablo said.

"All night," Jorge said. "So have I. I just woke up over there." He pointed to the open side door in the kitchen where the sound of waves crashing, and the smell of the ocean crept inside Pablo's apartment.

"What happened to us?" Pablo searched for answers, noticing the bruises on Jorge's face.

"Ruggy almost killed us, that's what happened. We jumped him, but he's a luchador. He squashed us. I don't remember who went down first. I took a hit, so did you. Jucélia ran. I think Ruggy left with Renata."

"We have to find them," Pablo said. "Can you take me to El Camarón? Jucélia's there. I know she is."

"My car's all the way at my place. Let's take yours," Jorge said.

Pablo patted his chest and shorts pockets. "Wait! My keys!" He ran to the nightstand in his bedroom where he always kept them, but they were gone. "He took my keys," Pablo shouted. "Ruggy took my keys!"

Jorge had since stepped out of the side door to the area where Pablo parked his Bronco.

"Your car is gone, too," he shouted to Pablo. "He must have taken it."

"No, Jucélia has it. I gave her instructions."

"How long have you two been . . . whatever is going on between you?"

"Is it that obvious?"

"Come on, cousin, everyone knows. I'm surprised Ruggy didn't kill you sooner."

"Let's go. I'll explain."

Before they stepped out, Pablo touched the carved Virgen de Guadalupe above the kitchen doorway. It was a gift from Claudia when his parents had passed away, and he often forgot the Blessed Mother was there. Today, he noticed her, watching him, and that small touch let her know he was watching her, too.

Once out of town in Jorge's car, the cousins pieced the night together. There was trouble brewing all along, and everyone felt it. Pablo told Jorge everything: the building tension between Pablo and Jucélia, the kiss in the lobby, and his trips. Jorge knew a little about that, but not everything.

"*Carnal*, are you a peeper or something?" Jorge said, pulling into Claudia's lot.

"Look, my car is here." Pablo's face brightened. "And no, I told you. I have a gift, and I only looked in on her a couple of times."

"Well, don't come watching me when I'm alone."

"Shut up," Pablo said. "Now, listen, inside, we're going to make a plan. I have an idea for how we're going to stop Ruggy."

"Stop Ruggy?" Jorge laughed. "He'll kill us."

"No. We can outsmart him."

The two got out and stood in the yard.

"He's going to open that bar with or without us," Jorge said.

"He can do whatever he wants," Pablo said. "Look. Look up there."

Pablo pointed to a corona that encircled the sun in a hazy sky.

"What? Is that you flying around?"

Pablo whacked Jorge's chest. "No. The weather. Storm's coming."

Though neither were hers by blood, Claudia's doors were always open to her nephews, especially Pablo. She did have an affinity for Jorge though, because it was his father, Luis Garza, whom she had always loved. And it was Luis who had gone on to raise Pablo after his parents had passed away, even though Pablo's mother Eva, had wanted Claudia to raise Pablo.

Inside, the warmth of candles and the scents of oils and herbs greeted the men. The dark hallway leading to Claudia's living room was lined with pictures of saints and family members and bookshelves with her books on *curandería* and works of fiction. The two walked in with soft feet with respect to the quiet calm of her home.

"Nina?" Pablo said above a whisper. "It's me, Pablo."

"And Jorge."

At the far end of her living room lit by candles and glowing daylight at the edges of the curtain-covered windows, Claudia stood with her eyes closed, her hands with palms facing outward in front of her face. Just below her on her bodywork table lie Jucélia on her back. Pablo stood in the absolute silence and knew that Claudia was administering light from within herself onto Jucélia, a Japanese method Claudia had studied for many years, adapted to her own spirituality, and even used on him a few times. It was alignment, she had told him, of the energies inside.

Jucélia twitched, her head moving. "Pablo?" she said.

"Shhh," Claudia hushed her.

"He's here." Jucélia opened her eyes and turned to him, her eyes welling up.

Claudia fluttered her eyes open and looked over at Pablo, letting her hands down. "Oh, *mi'hijo,* what trouble you all are in."

"I see you met Jucélia," Pablo smiled at his madrina. He then turned to Jucélia, fixated on her beautiful yet sad face. "You made it here." His hand connecting with hers, their touch at last without fear.

"She came in the middle of the night," Claudia said. "I had no idea what was happening. I thought the authorities were coming for me."

"I'm so sorry, *nina,*" Pablo said.

"No, I understood immediately. I remembered her from after the memorial last year. I saw her at the Bungalows. I wondered who they were."

"Where's Renata?" Jucélia sat up.

"Jorge says she left with Ruggy," Pablo embraced Jucélia, the two of them clinging to each other the way they had been wanting to for so long.

"I think Ruggy took her," Jorge said.

"After you left, it was a nightmare. He knocked us out," Pablo said.

"Hide here for as long as you want," Claudia said.

"He's opening the bar tonight," Pablo said. "We have to stop him."

"Don't worry yourself with that," Claudia said.

"That's what I've been telling him," Jucélia said.

"We can't stay here forever," Jorge said.

"And we have to find Renata," Jucélia said.

"Everybody just calm down," Claudia said. "I was working on Jucélia, helping to release her anxiety. By the looks of you two, you need some work. Look at those bruises on your cheeks. And you both need haircuts."

"No, Nina," Pablo said. "We don't have time."

"There's always time. That man has no idea where we are, and he's not going anywhere if he's so proud of that bar. Now you two take your shirts off and go sit in the kitchen. Jucélia, you come with me."

Claudia had made cold compresses for the cousins to hold to their faces, while she took her scissors in her wrinkled fingers and began to clip. She began on Jorge first.

"Rub his shoulders," she instructed Jucélia pointing to Pablo. He knew what she was doing: giving Pablo and Jucélia the time to connect with each other. With Jucélia's fingers on his skin, the feeling was more electric than his out of body journeys.

"So what of this man?" Claudia said. "He's a *luchador*?"

"Was," Jucélia said. "He's from the United States, of course, a state called Michigan. He said he left there to start wrestling."

"But what really happened?" Claudia said.

"He dodged the draft and ran to Brazil. That's where we met."

"He ran away from his own country?" Jorge said. "I knew he was a coward."

Claudia clipped the last strands of Jorge's hair and combed it back. "Done," she said, moving onto Pablo. "Next."

"And then you all came to Mexico?" Claudia said.

"He wanted to join the *lucha libre*. He made it in, but it didn't last. He was always the villain and wanted to be the hero."

"He's exactly what he wants to be," Claudia said. "Fans love to hate villains, and villains love to love themselves. So, ignore him and let him love himself."

"So, we just ignore him?" Pablo said.

"Make him lose at his own game." Claudia clipped and combed. "You boys and your long hair."

"I want to confront him at the opening tonight," Pablo said. "In front of the whole town."

"How?" Jucélia said.

"Like Claudia said. We play his game, but we let him lose. In town, I know a shop that sells *lucha* masks."

"Cousin, I think I know what you're thinking," Jorge said.

"Be smart," Claudia said. "Don't do something stupid."

"You're coming with us," Pablo said.

"What's an old lady going to do?"

"Teach him to respect women," Pablo said.

"You all need some rest and time to think," Claudia said.

"Jorge, you stay here and help me clean up and make lunch. *Pobrecita* Cici," Claudia said turning her attention to Jucélia, tucking her hair behind her ear. "That man has been watching you like his prey. You're not a mouse, remember that, *mi'hija*. You two go sit and talk. Take a rest."

Pablo put his shirt back on, and for the first time, he felt free to be with the person he most wanted to be with.

Pablo led Jucélia through Claudia's home, showing pictures of him when he was younger, pictures of his parents, of Jorge. This walkabout was therapeutic for both of them, and it was most comforting for Pablo to be in what was his second home. It was here he had come once a week to practice guitar with Claudia, brought there by Tío Luis. It was there he had wanted to live after Claudia moved out of town and up into the hills.

"Your aunt loves you very much," Jucélia said.

"I think she loves you, too," Pablo said.

"I hardly know her," Jucélia said.

"She loves whomever I love."

"Are you saying ..." Jucélia's breath fell from under her words.

"I'm saying what we've been trying to say to each other for a while."

He took her hand and led her into Claudia's room, the very same room he had walked in as a boy after he had finished his solo lesson early and was wondering Claudia's home, looking for her and Luis, only to find them there, Tío Luis naked on his back, his hands holding Claudia's waist—she on top of him, hips moving forward and back over him, breathing deeply, her black hair flowing down to the curve of her back, hands on his uncle's chest.

"Ay, please go, *mi amor*," Claudia had said, covering herself with her arms. Tío Luis glanced over, eyes wide with guilt.

But here, now as a man and not a boy, Pablo felt no such guilt, and in that moment he sensed Jucélia felt no guilt either. With the door closed, they continued the embrace they had started in the lobby of the Bungalows, which then led to the kiss they had started but had to stop. Although now, that kiss continued and went on, further and with more passion, until they were lost in one another.

After, they held to each other, realizing that there was indeed time. Tía Claudia was right. It was then that Pablo told Jucélia of his power.

"I saw you a couple of times, and I wanted to save you so badly then," he said.

"The strangest part is," she said, "I felt you. I felt your presence. It's like you really are an angel."

"Let's rest now," he whispered. "Like Claudia said."

And there they closed their eyes to sleep, for the first time as a couple.

Slip Soul by Joe DeVries
Chapter 13

During their nap, Pablo drifted again out of his body shooting out of himself like a bolt, then morphing into a sphere of energy. He had a few of these in his life, and they were always when he was in a happy mood. In a peaceful embrace with a new love in the home of his godmother, his spirit was free to fly. And he soared over the ocean, his form blasting upward and down, skimming over water with the sweeping Puerto Escondido beach and hills ahead of him.

His electric ball of energy reshaped into a human form the moment he drew closer to the beach and the Bungalows, and near there, Paradiso. Ruggy toiled in the midday sun arranging the bar for opening night. Zooming in for a closer view, Pablo saw the bottles of alcohol under the bar, clean cups and glasses, and a keg of beer. Ruggy was testing the music system-a simple stereo with a cord running back toward Calle del Morro. At one point, Ruggy and Pablo agreed that Pablo was going to play there hoping to bring the crowds from La Sirena to Paradiso.

Pablo's form flew once more around the bar, and he was simply going to fly away until he glimpsed the plastic diamond of his key chain hanging out of Ruggy's pocket. The bastard had stolen them. His calm energy zapped into a fury and his spirt form whizzed around the bar, stirring up the hanging lamps and rustling the leaves of the palapa. Pablo had found ways to make contact with the physical world in this form, yet it was never enough to do more than what he was doing then. Simple movements like the push of a picture frame or the moving of papers on a desk.

But here, facing Ruggy in spirit form, Pablo went at him, gathering all of his energy and focusing on Ruggy's chest. Aimed at the wrestler, Pablo charged into him. The hit worked, sending Ruggy backward, catching himself before he fell to the floor. The keys jiggled out of his pocket and Pablo went to try to reach them, but he had no grasp, plus, he felt weakened by the hit to Ruggy. His frame of view went dark, and a blurry vision replaced the brightness of the beach.

Flashes of an enclosed space appeared along with an outline of a body in distress. Pablo sensed it was Renata. The vision vanished and Pablo's form hovered again at Paradiso. Ruggy stood and took the keys, tucking them back into his pocket. He looked around nervously and called out, "Who's there?"

Pablo knew he had to leave, but before he left, he gave Ruggy another sign. As he flew up and around the bar, Pablo pushed his energy toward the palapa, shaking all the leaves and causing Ruggy to look up in fear.

"Who's there?" he shouted again.

Pablo headed for the shed. He knew that's what the vision was telling him. Once he had vaporized through the wooden doors, he saw and heard Renata. She was tied up in a corner by the tarps. She moaned; her energy depleted. Ruggy truly was a madman. Pablo tried to soothe her, sending warmth to her, but this would not help. Rescuing her would. This realization sent his spirt form hurtling back to his living body next to Jucélia in Claudia's home.

He came to and sprang up. "She's in the shed!" he said, waking Jucélia. "Renata's in the shed."

Jucélia fluttered her eyes and started to cry. "We must go to her. Now."

On their way down the hill, Jucélia riding with Pablo, and Claudia riding with Jorge, they stopped at the tourist shop Pablo had mentioned. In addition to the wooden puppets and necklaces made of leather and rice, they sold *luchador* accessories. Shirts commemorating your favorite *técnico* and capes belonging to your hated *rudo*.

And masks of every kind. Pablo bought several of them, enough to form a squad of fighters.

"Jorge and I will get Renata," Pablo said before they continued on into Zicatela. "I want you two to go back into my apartment and hide."

"I'm going with you to get my sister," Jucélia said.

"But we have to be careful. Ruggy cannot see you. He's can't see any of us."

"Let's just go," Jucélia pleaded. "Let's get her now."

Back at the Bungalows, Pablo and Jorge made sure to park away from the building, then they led Jucélia and Claudia through the back way of the Bungalows and had Jorge stay with them in a small open shed where Gustavo the gardener kept his tools and fertilizers.

"Wait here," Pablo said.

On the patio, two long-haired surfers sat a table drinking beer. They turned to him. "Are you Pablo?" one said.

Pablo caught his breath, "Yes."

"The sign on the door says to call Pablo about checking in. We want to check in."

Pablo held up his finger. "Pick a room. Do you mind if they're not made up? I've been away."

They shrugged and lifted up their bags and boards.

Pablo turned the knob to the lobby door. Locked.

"Guys, have you seen the surf?"

He pointed out to the sea, and with their eyes in the other direction, Pablo tilted the big jade plant in the red pot and prayed the spare was there. It shone back at him, and he thanked God for that blessed talisman no one else knew was there.

It only opened the front door, which gave access to his apartment unit behind the desk; not the units, the shed, or the safe. He unlocked the lobby, bent down to collect the pile of keys and envelopes of check-out money.

"Come on in, *señores*," he said, pushing the old leather-bound register to them before getting behind the desk. He scanned the board for vacated rooms.

"Here," he said. "Number three. Two doubles. I'll give a discount because the housekeeper is off. Is that okay?"

"Fine by us." They shrugged. "We just want to hit the surf."

"Where you two from?" Pablo said.

"The States," one of them answered.

"Oh, yeah?" Pablo said, "You know there's a big party tonight. You should go. It's going to be big, lots of women and a special performance."

"We will," one said.

"Free drinks, too. Ask for Ruggy. He's American, just like you." Pablo said.

The surfers left the lobby and Pablo emptied the envelopes, shoved the cash in his pocket. He hung up the keys on the board and ran into his unit to get an extra tool kit he kept there. Back at the gardener's shed, he sent Claudia to his apartment and told her to wait for the knock.

"Let's go get Renata," he told Jucélia and Jorge.

By the shed, the fronds of the tall palms flapped in the breeze, accompanied by a noticeable chill as the afternoon had begun to wither away. The shed door was shut and locked just as he imagined, but he drove the sharp end of a screwdriver into the lock, then slammed the top with a hammer. After a few blows, the lock came apart and he was able to pull the door open.

The three stepped forward into the darkened shed. Pablo reached for a flashlight he knew was on the tool bench once inside. He aimed the feeble yellow beam toward the tarps in the corner, and there was Renata, blindfolded with two pieces of silver duct tape crossed in an X over her mouth, hands tied behind her back, and slumped against the back wall. They ran to her, falling to their knees to wake her. Jucélia pulled off her blindfold and Renata's eyes blinked back to life. She was scared, pleading to them in silence to help her. Jorge untied her hands and held on as Pablo braced her as he pulled off the tape.

She sucked in air and sobbed, and scooted herself toward them, her whole body quaking as she threw her arms out to them.

"Oh, *irmã*," Jucélia embraced her sister, smoothing her in her arms. "What did he do to you?"

Renata, in her underpants and a *camiseta*, cried and held Jucélia closer.

"Come," Pablo said, "let's go to my apartment and take care of you, get you cleaned up. We can't stay here."

Pablo and Jorge helped Renata to her feet, with Jucélia supporting her the whole way. The group walked her quickly down the passage toward the lobby where a cool breeze followed them inside. Once behind the desk and at his apartment door, Pablo knocked with the special taps, and Claudia opened the door an inch and peeked at them, then opened the door wide and ushered them quickly inside.

12 - LA JOLLA

"I'M NERVOUS FOR THEM," MARCOS SAYS. "It's like they're scared in their own country."

"That's exactly how we are right now, hijo. We are in the country of Lester Brooks. It was once good to cross over here. My son was right. I think now I'm ready to tell you how I ended up here, right here.

"I woke up in the storeroom of Hugo and Beatriz with light coming through the vertical blinds waking me earlier than I wanted. Though I was rested, I awoke with a distinct sense of worry. I shook off that feeling by quickly getting ready for work in the small washroom and remembering that I still had at least two new friends in Hugo and Beatriz. They knocked to make sure I was awake.

"'Here,' Hugo said and handed me a phone. 'My number is programmed under my name. Call us. See you this afternoon,' they said.

"Those people were saints," Marcos says.

"In every way . . . Later, I arrived to the Beyer station and the north bound trolley had just left. I would be a little late. With it being Tamale Thursday at Sea of Cortez, my job was to meet Tony Sandoval, the tamalero that brought the tamales to the store. That was one of the few things Sea of Cortez did right. I hoped Artie Sanchez would not be upset with me running behind.

"Once off the trolley at the Mission Center stop, there was a row of stores along a narrow parking lot full of cars. Those buildings and the shoppers inside reminded me that everything in that part of town was about comfort. Sandwiches, frozen yogurt, large reclining chairs, and mattresses. Up ahead was the yellow restaurant called *On the Border* where it looked like they were trying to make every day Cinco de Mayo, if only they knew what Cinco de Mayo was. I picked up my feet crossing the street to go to Sea of Cortez. I thought that would be the day for Artie Sanchez and me to talk about what to do next. He once said, 'Don't worry Osvaldo, we'll talk about your options.' In the United States, they're always talking about their options.

"At the corner of Camino de La Reina and Camino Del Este, the light stopped me. Being a few minutes late I thought I could blend in. It was the shift before the store opened. Artie never seemed to get angry, just very focused. He would understand that the old man might need a little more time. The green and yellow lights of the Subway restaurant shined in the mid-morning light along with a different light, spinning and flashing red and yellow. Something wasn't right. The lights were on top of a car. It was the police—the black and white I recognized. There were other cars, large, tall vehicles, not black and white, but green striped with yellow lights. Imigración.

"Everything inside me beginning at my stomach froze, then traveled outward. My lungs stopped, even my eyes, and limbs. The pounding of my blood was the only reminder I was still alive. Artie Sanchez was pushed into the police car with his hands in cuffs behind his back. The officers in brown uniforms took Pinche Tomás and shoved him into their car. Other workers, some of the men I knew and saw once in a while were both grabbed and folded like paper into the cars.

"Young Ernesto was there, standing and watching. He was the only safe Mexican. And there was Daisy in her Sea of Cortez uniform. She was by the side door, observing, not moving. It was hard to see her face or her expression, but she was still, like a statue, and appeared to be in shock herself about what was happening. She was next to a big man, also watching the scene. I watched it from afar, stunned, with nothing I could do about it. The man next to Daisy was familiar in a strange way. Was he a customer? He and Daisy talked. They were close. Maybe related. I thought it must be her father. He was an older white man, large and mean looking. Was he showing her what her job would be like?

"There was no time to think any more about it. There was enough space between the nightmare over there and the reality that this was it—the end. Time to go, get away as fast as I could. Just get behind the tall office building in the parking lot, back away, don't stumble, turn away, walk fast. Run. Running like that was not a natural act anymore. It was awkward and a little clumsy for me. The weight felt unbalanced, joints out of alignment. Something in my thigh, began to ache.

"Across the street at the mall, the big stores and movie theaters were a refuge. I thought about mixing in with crowds or getting lost in a store. Even sitting in the darkness of a movie theater. But if la migra was just at Sea of Cortez, they could go to the movies. There were police everywhere in the city. And the mall could not be that much safer. In the United States, gunmen walk in anywhere and shoot everyone. Schools. Churches. Movie theaters.

"All I could do was sit on a bench to catch my breath. I opened my bag and reached for the phone Hugo had given me that morning. I called him and asked for another helping hand. He said to find a coffee shop and stay there until he could come get me. He arrived a couple of hours later and brought me back to San Ysidro.

"'They're everywhere,' I told him on the car ride back. 'It's like they know I'm running out of time. My visa ran out today.'

"That night, I went back home with Hugo, we all had dinner again, and I relaxed somewhat with a good meal and the idea that I would have another night's sleep without threats. Back in the storeroom, before I went to sleep, Hugo gave me a small plastic bag and a hanger with a shirt."

"'Here, I brought you some nice clothes. You can't go to La Jolla looking like you work at a taco stand, at Sea of Cortez.'

"In the bag was some worn, but nice black leather shoes and a pair of dress pants. On the hanger was a sky-blue dress shirt. My face twisted up again and I tried not to bite my lip.

"'But are these yours? No, I can't.

"'We're about the same size,' Hugo said. And take these shoes. You need to look nice for her. Women like a man with nice shoes. But you know that already.”

“'Thank you for taking this poor pilgrim into your home. I can see that you and Bea have helped so many people.”

“'Relax tonight.' He rested his hand on my shoulder. 'Empty your mind.'

“All I could say was thank you.

“'And tomorrow, take your time. Sleep late. Bea will make breakfast for you and then we will drive you to La Jolla. We'll leave in the afternoon.'

“As I drifted to sleep that night I thought of the raid at Sea of Cortez. I hated to think I was the reason Artie Sanchez was caught. Was I? I worried where he was or what they did to him. I thought they might have closed Sea of Cortez, that everyone would have lost their job. And I thought about Daisy, how she just stood there. *What if she had joined Immigration?* What were they training her to do? The next day, I found out.

“It was Daisy, wasn't it?” Marcos asks.

I look around the infirmary room, hoping to find a window to look out, and just as it feels as though it's getting warmer, the cold air blasts again.

“Yes, it was Daisy. She was undercover the whole time.

“That afternoon, we were delayed leaving San Ysidro. Hugo was waiting for his other manager to come mind the store and Beatriz had been on a phone call. Once I was in the back of their nice SUV, I felt like a teenager with my parents driving me to a school dance. Beatriz spoke fast to keep me occupied and not worried that we were late and cutting into Joanne's reading.

“'We'll be fine,' she said. 'La Jolla is small, once we get there, we'll just park and find a seat.'

“'But the parking, Bea,' Hugo said.

“People are always talking about parking in California, by the way.

“'Is it free? Did we find that out?' Bea said. She looked at her phone to find out. 'Oh yes, it is. It is free. Should we sit together?'

“'I think Osvaldo might want to go in by himself,' Hugo said.

Beatriz turned back to me. 'Osvaldo, do you want to go in by yourself?'

I was lost in my thoughts, my mind racing as I watched the city pass by in a blur. I could feel the change from the needy south to the abundant north, the move toward all the food, water, and resources. It wasn't like San Ysidro and Tijuana, two giant but different cities back-to-back. It was all within the same place, though there was an obvious difference between the parts of the city.

"'Yes,' I said. 'If you don't mind. I'll go to the reading alone.'

"LA JOLLA WAS JUST WHAT I imagined, a jewel by the sea. It hangs there, almost ready to fall in, like a big diamond on a woman's knuckle. It sparkles in ordinary daylight, and it's much cooler than the rest of San Diego. Far off the coast, a thick fog gathered, heading straight for the caves below them. On the bluffs above the caves, pine trees bent to the West, worshipping the sea, their spines twisted and curved in prayer, or penitence.

"There was nothing there like where I lived or where I worked. There was no Sea of Cortez or Subway. It was all cafes, pastries, sushi and athletic clothes. The wealthy love all of those small things that fit into your mouth in one bite, so that they can then put on those matching exercise clothes. But did they exercise? They should look happier if they did. Most of them seemed to be in some kind of pain. Maybe in their heads, as though it hurt so much to live in a place with that much beauty.

"Once Hugo and Beatriz dropped me off at the store—it was the last time I saw them—I was too late. At the closed glass doors looking in, I caught a glimpse of Joanne, thin and elegant as I thought she would be, her hair naturally grayed and pulled up into a bun. She stood in front of the seated group of mostly viejos like me, except they were all white. White hair, white skin, white teeth, white clothes. I wasn't going to fit in if I tried. I pulled the door handle and as if on cue, they all clapped for Joanne and began standing and gathering their things.

"A man spoke over everyone, telling them to enjoy the wine and thanking them for coming, as he pointed to a table of books where he stood next to Joanne.

154

"'Please get your copy,' he said. "She'll be here signing. Thank you again, Joanne. It was lovely.'

"I thought that was her husband, and I almost walked out. I almost lost all the courage I had built up. I could have walked out with my bag that had her manuscript in it, called my parents Hugo and Bea to come pick me up."

"But you didn't, did you?" Marcos says.

"No, I worked my way through that crowd of old people and found the line. Some studied the cover, others fluttered open the pages. Some who already had their copy had formed the line at the table where she sat. Each of them waited to get time—any time with her. And I could see why. It was her smile, how her calm told you everything was going to be fine. I had enough cash to buy a copy. I picked one up and held it with the same love and care as I did her first copy. There it was, *Slip Soul,* Stories and a Novella by Joanne Watson McCasey. I thumbed the pages looking for the name I knew, Pablo Garza. The character she based on me.

"As the line moved closer to Joanne, I admit I felt bad for going. Why was I intruding on her world without a warning? What kind of gentleman am I? But the man who spoke at the end was no longer near her, and he didn't seem like he was hers. And as I got closer, I did not see a ring on her thin fingers. She signed books and kept smiling, and nodded her head, and as she did that, the girl I met under the lamp in the zócalo came back in my mind. How she was fascinated by everything around her, yet how scared she was behind her own eyes. How she held onto me with that look, like I belonged to her. Like she was mine, too.

"I stepped forward. Two people in front of me. They seemed to take a long time. It was then I thought I should have left. Wasn't seeing her enough? I could have left and been satisfied. Then there was one person left in line, then me. The store had almost cleared out. I had stayed until the end. And then it was me. The last to approach her table.

"I moved ahead and set her original words on the small table in front of her, the pages bent and frayed, the gold brads still holding it all together, the paper and fading ink I had cherished for more than three decades.

She tilted her head to the side, lay her hand over her heart. She smiled and her chin quivered. My stomach, like on that wild Himalaya carnival ride

Felipe used to drag me on every year during the Guelaguetza, dropped as far as it could go, then lifted back up with a warmth that electrified my entire insides. She was there, right in front of me, and I smiled back as I had only smiled once in my life—that first night we met in the zócalo in Oaxaca City, two souls, at last, aligned.

"'Osvaldo. Is that you?' She stood and came around from the signing table.

"'Hola, Juana. It's me.'

"'Well, what are you doing—how, I . . .'"

"'I know, I know. I'm in town. I'm visiting. I work in the US and heard about this.'

'Come here.' She pulled me into her, and I felt her again in my arms.

We hadn't been that close since we were both in Ensenada—Motel California—our bodies surrendering to one another as it was meant to happen.

"'I can't believe it's you,' she said over and again. 'This is impossible.'

"She was like a work of art I couldn't stop admiring. It was impossible to me, too.

"The man I thought was her husband lingered near us but knew to give us space. He took the "Author Signing" event sign down and replaced it with the "Closed" sign. He hung around, waiting for an answer.

"'Bill, Bill,' she said. 'This is—one of my oldest friends.' Joanne took my hand, that feeling. 'Osvaldo Reyes. From Oaxaca.'

"We reached for each other's hands.

"'Mr. McCasey?' I said.

"'Oh, no, no,' he said, 'this is my shop.'

"'I'm sorry,' I said.

"'Nice to meet you, Osvaldo.'

"'Mucho gusto.'

"'Thank you Bill, this night was perfect.' Joanne hugged him.

"'You sold a lot of books,' he said.

"'You're my best store. Always have been.'

"'You two have a lot of catching up to do, I'm sure,' Bill said. 'Enjoy the night.'

"Joanne and I pushed the front glass doors open. Bill Duncan closed and locked them behind us. Pink clouds drifted in under the purple sky of evening, and there, in the mild air blanketing us, Joanne's nearness giving equal, if not more comfort, we stepped outside the store, together.

"We held each other's hands by our sides. It was a dream—all of it.

"'There's a place, just down here, it's a coffee shop. Let's go there. Let's talk,' she said.

"'No one else with you?'

"She looked aside but smiled. 'Just us. I came alone.'

"Finally, it felt right. It felt like my whole life had been building toward that moment.

"I went with her, holding her, but not holding her, our bodies touching and then not, our arms and hands reaching, brushing each other's skin, the fabric of our clothes. We almost tripped over each other. My heart thumped in my chest, my mouth taking in more air than my lungs allowed.

"One of the parked cars along the curb turned off its lights, two people stepped out. In my world with Joanne, I paid them no attention, until one of them, the woman of the pair, walked forward to us, as though she knew me. For a moment I thought it was Hugo and Bea, but it was Daisy from work. I was happy to see her. Maybe she was planning to come to the reading, too.

"I bet she was planning to go," Marcos said.

"'Daisy!' I reached out for her. 'You're here. You came. This is Joanne.'

"Joanne stopped and held my arm, pulled me back.

"'Look, I found her.' I said to Daisy.

"Behind Daisy was a man—he was familiar. He approached us fast, the way Daisy did. But she was cold, not the girl from Sea of Cortez.

"'Joanne, this is Daisy.'

"'I knew I would find you here,' Daisy said, and she yanked me forward into what I thought would be a hug, but she gripped my forearm and twisted my arm behind me, hooking it into my back. She signaled to the man with her. I remembered him—it was the man from the day before outside the Sea of Cortez.

"He took over, grabbed my other arm, and I searched for Daisy, her head bobbed, moving around me. She ripped my bag off my shoulders. Joanne had inserted herself into this takeover, pushing the man away, yelling at Daisy to stop.

"'Ma'am,' she said to Joanne. 'Stand down.'

"She wasn't Daisy in those moments. She had turned into someone else.

"The man pulled Joanne away.

"'He's my friend,' Joanne said. 'Stop it. What did he do? He's not a criminal.'

"'Daisy, why? Why you doing this?'

"'I have to do my job. You have to go back to your country.'

"'But Daisy, I'm going back. Leave me alone, please.'

"The man had both of my hands behind me now, my wrists pinched into a plastic tie.

"'As an alien with an overstayed visa, U.S. Immigration and Customer Enforcement is required to bring you to justice, sir.'

"Daisy repeated everything in perfect Spanish. Neither were in uniform. Just their regular clothes. She'd been hiding all along but leaving clues. How stupid I was not to pay attention—and to tell her my life story the way I did. Why didn't she just take me then?

"'Do you two feel better about yourselves. Do you feel like a man?' Joanne stood in the man's face.

"'Mi mochila, take it, Joanne,' I pointed at the ground to my bag.

"Joanne reached for my bag, but Daisy grabbed it. She opened it up as though she were ripping open the bags of lettuce at Sea of Cortez. I'd often thought she had a mean side, but how could she, as sweet as she was. She dumped it open onto the sidewalk. The manuscript and my new copy of Joanne's book hit the concrete. My whole life spilled onto the sidewalk, shimmering under the streetlamp in La Jolla.

"Daisy shuffled through my things, then kicked the bag toward Joanne.

"'What is your name?' Joanne collected the remains, dusted off the manuscript and book, the phone given to me by the Los López. She stood and got close to Daisy's face.

"'Agent Desiree Baca,' Daisy said.

'You don't treat people like this. You don't treat a senior citizen like this. An innocent man.'

"Daisy's partner had pulled me back toward the car they stepped out from. It was a large truck. A cell on wheels. The man tugged and jerked me away and into the vehicle.

"Daisy left Joanne, who started running after us, toward the car, screaming, pleading.

"'No, no, no, please, he's my friend. Stop this.'

"Daisy shot me a look like she was at the cash register, and I was in the back at the chip hopper, like she might send me an order or correct me—tell me to call the totopos chips. Chips. That she could speak perfect Spanish all along like this hurt my stomach.

"'I'm sorry, Osvaldo. I liked you. But you know the laws. Discúlpame.'

"'You're not to apologize to them,' The man corrected Daisy.

"Joanne banged on the windshield and hood as Daisy and her partner drove off. A sourness took over my mouth and the wetness of sweat and tears on my face blurred my eyes. I felt like I had just been kicked, or sliced, or pierced by an arrow in the ankle, unable to bite something like the butt of my fist to combat the pain. All I could do was hold some of it in, letting go of the ache in tiny exhales as small toxic vapors escaping my nose."

"OSVALDO, OH MY GOD," Marcos says. "Now I know why you've been keeping that all inside of you. They were hunting you. She was hunting you. That is horrible."

I shrug. "What could I do? It's over now."

"Joanne is looking for you," Marcos says. "She at least knows where you are. She sent you the letter. And her book. She's coming for you. She has to."

"I hope. Here. I'll read the last chapters to you before we have to go back to work."

Slip Soul by Joe DeVries
Chapter 14

Evening had fallen, and after Jucélia and Claudia had cared for Renata in the bathroom for an extended time, the group gathered in the living area, where just the night before the truth had been revealed.

Now cleaned and dressed, Renata was exhausted and still tearful. She only wanted to lay on the sofa with her eyes closed. It seemed she and Jucélia had spoken at length in the bathroom, and now they needed time apart. Pablo sensed this, and though he didn't want to meddle, this was their moment to act.

"Our plan is to drive right up to the bar and shine the lights on it," Pablo said. "Jorge's going to start the show. Right, Jorge?"

Jorge nodded and smiled. He was ready, though the girls were not.

"We will all wear masks," Pablo said.

"I'm not going," Renata said. "I'm not doing whatever it is you're planning."

"We face him together," Pablo said. "All of us."

"She's—" Jucélia paused. "She's not going."

"What happened, Nata?" Pablo said. "You can tell us. We're safe here."

Claudia moved toward Renata. She put one hand on Renata's head, and the other on her heart. "Go ahead, mi'hija. You can say."

Renata turned her body toward the wall and cried. Claudia patted her back, and Jucélia came over to tend to her, too. Once Renata calmed, she turned around to face them all. She wiped her face then sat up. She began by looking at her sister.

"All my life, I've looked up to you, *irmã*, and it's funny, because you're the younger sister. But you're smarter and prettier, and you always get what you want."

"*Irmã*, that's not true. You're beautiful and smart, too."

"Yes, you are," Jorge said.

"Last night, after everything happened, you just took off. You left me. You left me there. I figured you and Pablo had some plan. I watched Ruggy destroy everything, and a little part of me was happy to see him do it. I know he's a bad man, but I just let him, because in that moment, I was alone. And I thought, why not? Why not him and me? You know that even at the beginning, I had eyes for him, and he had eyes for you. Like it always is.

"I thought I might calm him after you had left and after the boys were passed out. I tried to talk him into going home, that maybe you were there. You weren't, and he went deeper into his rage. We came back here, and that was when he grabbed your keys, Pablo. I thought then I would run because I knew he was acting wild, but that's when he got me. He took me back to our place and he cornered me. He made me confess that I knew about the flirting between you two. But he already knew. He'd read your diary, like he said at the party. He just wanted me to say it, too, and that made him even more angry. It made him crazy that we were all against him. I don't blame him."

She paused, looked at everyone.

"But," she said, "it's still wrong. He's still a terrible man and he needs to be stopped. I just don't want to do it, because last night, after he tried to force himself on me and I fought him off—you see these bruises— and while he was dragging me to the shed to lock me up, he said he would kill all of you once he saw you again."

"Why didn't he come back in here and just finish us off?" Jorge said.

"I told him not to. I reminded him of his business. That he had to open it the next day," Renata said.

"You saved us all," Jucélia said. "I tried to bring you, remember, but I had to run. I know I should have never left you there. That was wrong, and I'm so sorry."

"I still love you," Renata said. "I understand why you did what you did. What he did to me is nothing compared to what he does to you. I can't stand to see him hurt you all the time."

"Then now is your chance." Claudia stood in front of the girls. "If you want to support your sister, redeem your dignity, and get rid of that mother fucker, now is the time."

Pablo had never heard his godmother use that kind of language, but he liked it. He stood up and shouted in agreement.

"We'll all be together," Pablo said. "He can't hurt all of us at once."

"I won't let him hurt you," Jorge said, taking Renata's hand. "Never again."

Jucélia embraced her sister once more and after more quiet tears, they let go and Renata stood.

"What's the plan?" she asked.

Slip Soul by Joe DeVries
Chapter 15

The group met one more time in the darkened lobby of the Bungalows. Pablo and Jorge peeked out of the picture window that faced the *malecón*. Paradiso had flickered to life. The strings of clear bulbs that hung under the palapa formed a bright web as forceful American rock and roll blasted from the speaker. Ruggy never wanted Mexican or reggae music. From that distance, the place didn't look so bad. A tiny swell of pride rose up in Pablo, though he squashed it just as fast, knowing it was never about him. Plus, you can't build paradise. It just is.

"Masks on," Pablo said.

The group pulled their masks over their heads and gave each other strong hugs of encouragement.

Back in Pablo's apartment, they went over the plan.

"Are you sure this will work," Jucélia said to Pablo.

"It's the only way. He has to pay for what he did to you and Renata. He'll get the message, and then he'll leave."

"I love you," she said, and kissed him through his mask.

They stepped out of the lobby and into a brisk breeze in the night sky. The weather had indeed turned from the heat of summer to a threatening storm just off the coast.

With the lights off, Jorge drove Pablo's Bronco ahead onto the sand and waited. The music from the stereo speaker Ruggy had set up matched the jerky movement of the guests drinking beer, taking shots, lighting cigarettes and puffing smoke out, throwing their heads back, laughing. All the seats around the bar were full with the tanned locals and the young, lithe tourists of all colors, mostly reddened by sun. Swarms of people formed a ring around those seated, elbowing their way up to the bar. La Sirena hadn't seen nights like that in a while.

Ruggy worked double time behind the bar. He wore a red and gold, chest-hugging shirt with his old stage name printed on the back from sleeve to sleeve. RUGGER. He'd messed his hair that night, or what he could mess since it was so short. It wasn't perfectly straight up and angled with his tub of greasy pomade. Either he didn't have time to primp, or he was playing another part, this time bar owner with a bunch of fancy alcohol. No one in Playa Zicatela wants a whiskey sour. Come on. They want an ice-cold beer and a warm shot of mezcal.

More people had arrived: guests from the Bungalows,

friends of Pablo and Jorge, more locals, even a police officer, Cárdenas, who had befriended Ruggy because he was a *lucha libre* fan. All were the perfect audience for what was to come. It seemed they had settled into the mix with a desire, more than anything, to satisfy curiosity. While Ruggy took their money, Jauncho Navarro, a worker from Los Tíos restaurant and one of Ruggy's few friends, helped fill mugs and slide them out to the drinkers.

An offshore gust whipped the bar, and the women, wrapped in gauzy tops and lacy shawls huddled into each other, or their men, for protection. A sprinkle of rain began. Just then, Pablo gave the signal to Jorge. Jorge turned on his high beams and drove the Bronco ahead leaving enough space between them and the bar for the performance. Ruggy and Jauncho shielded their eyes. Engine revving, then lowering, a loud, gritty song erupted from the Bronco cutting into the tropical beat. A raspy Australian man's voice matched the rip of electric guitars.

Dirty deeds, it sang. Done dirt cheap. It was Ruggy's entrance song to the ring; the one that brought audiences to their feet either to boo or worship him. Jorge jumped out of his truck and clapped to the beat. He rocked back and forth, his head, covered in a luchador mask. The guests picked it up with ease.

Ruggy threw the towel off his shoulder onto the bar and stepped toward the sand. "Jorge?"

Jorge played an invisible guitar with the music, marching forward. He faced Ruggy. "Who wants to see the Rugger From Down Under in action?"

Ruggy waved it off. "No, no, no, folks. Rugger's retired. Just relax." He leaned toward Jorge. "What in the hell are you doing?"

"Come on!" Jorge clapped. "Who wants to see the Rugger from Down Under in action? Come on. *¡Ándale!*"

He clapped harder and started the chant, Ru-ggy! Ru-ggy! Ru-ggy! Until a chorus of the luchador's name echoed back at him. Jorge whispered to Ruggy, "Come on, man, this is for you. It's a celebration. Go with it."

"Wh—who am I up against?" A smile had spread across Ruggy's face. In the light of the high beams, feet planted now in the sand, the guy looked more at home than he ever had been in Playa Zicatela. He was back on stage, ready to wrestle.

"We got it, we got it," Jorge said. "Here," he pulled off his mask and tossed it to Ruggy. "Put this on. Go wait over there by the lights."

"Seriously, Jorge, what's going on?" Ruggy caught the mask. "Is that Pablo's Bronco?"

Jorge kept the crowd going. Ru-ggy! Ru-ggy! Ru-ggy! He moved under the palapa and sidled up next to Juancho, who was glowing with pride.

"In honor of the new bar, Paradiso," Jorge shouted, "The Rugger from Down Under is going to show us what he can do in the ring. Aren't you, Ruggy?"

The crowd clapped and whistled. Jorge chanted with the crowd.

"But who?" Ruggy slipped the mask over his head. The crowd cheered.

The song ended, and the moment it started to play again, a bolt cracked across the sky. A moment later, the sprinkle turned into rain. The clapping stopped, replaced by gasps, and the Rugger From Down Under stood before his people, in his scowling mask, arms flexed at his sides.

"The Rugger from Down Under is known to hurt people," Jorge said. "He's a punisher."

The passenger door of the Bronco opened. Jucélia, Renata, and Claudia, each masked and caped, their costumes glittering in the rain, stepped out and into view of the patrons.

"What is this?" Ruggy shouted at Jorge.

"And the people he punishes most are women," Jorge said. "Meet Jucélia and Renata. Two sisters from Brazil.

He treats them both like they're his property. Don't you, Ruggy?"

The sisters stepped forward and crouched into a fighting stance.

"Officer Cárdenas," Jorge shouted. "Ruggy kidnapped Renata here and locked her up. Didn't you, Ruggy?"

Cárdenas shot Ruggy a look of surprise. Ruggy shrugged it off. Drinks were set down. Cigarettes stubbed out. The wind now kicked with a mean intent, rustling the leaves of the palapa. Another bolt broke across the sky, and the crash of a wave—now closer to Paradiso—drowned the sound of Jorge's voice.

Ruggy shoved Jorge. "What are you doing? Stop this!"

"If he abused these two women, what's stopping him from hurting an old lady?" Jorge started his clap again. "Come on, everybody. Ru-ggy! Ru-ggy! Ru-ggy!"

Tía Claudia stepped forward and posed in a fighting stance.

Some patrons jumped off their stools and turned to leave. But most got back into it and clapped back along with Jorge. The women linked arms and stood three strong. On Claudia's count, they removed their masks.

"Lester," Jucélia said. "We're through. Go home. Go back to the U.S."

"And take your awful music with you." Renata spit on the sand. "You coward."

Just then, Pablo stepped forward.

"Ruggy," he said, "you used me for everything. This whole place is because of what I gave you. What I handed to you."

Ruggy lurched forward to go at Pablo, but Pablo stopped him with his words.

"I don't want to fight you, Lester. I want you to apologize for how you treated these women."

By then, the remaining guests began to boo. They slapped the bar chiding Ruggy all while the weather worsened by the minute.

"Take your mask off, too," Pablo said. "You're a fake."

Jorge began with a different chant. The chant that destroys rudos in the ring. *Desenmascarar.* Unmask. The crowd joined in until Ruggy stood there humiliated and furious.

The rain had turned into a downpour and the wind began swirling around them. The guests picked up to leave, and Ruggy leapt at Pablo, but he dodged him and in doing so, he grabbed the mask off of Ruggy's head.

"Get back to the car!" Pablo shouted ushering Jorge and the women to the Bronco.

"Come!" Jucélia said, grabbing Pablo's hand.

Ruggy had sprung up and was moving toward them. The waves had begun to crash nearer to them, growing stronger, hitting the beach harder and more often. The sea was rising around their ankles.

"Get to safety," Pablo said, shutting the door to his Bronco.

"No, Pablo, come with us," Jucélia pleaded.

"I have to finish this," he said. "Now, go!"

Jorge drove away with them, and now it was Ruggy and Pablo left on the beach. The wind howled while rain fell harder on them.

"Apologize," Pablo shouted. "To them and to yourself."

A set of waves rushed up around them, lifting them into the sea.

"I never liked you anyway," Ruggy said. "You dumb Mex—"

Ruggy's words were knocked out of him as the wind ripped the palapa cover away plucking the four posts of what had been the support beams of Paradiso. One of them smashed onto Ruggy pulling him under into the rising sea.

It had been years since Pablo had been in the water. He'd avoided it following his parents' deaths. He remembered how it traveled up the ankles, bathing the shins and thighs, then loins. How it rose up over your chest, and then to your neck until you were fully under.

He used to love it, then it terrified him. It was like the sensation of crossing over to the other side, of the soul leaving the body, as it had done just now.

He floated above the water, looking down on the storm. He knew he would soon zap back into himself as he had always done now that this was over with Ruggy. Now that the evil had been removed from his world. But his body wasn't in view on the ocean anymore. The Pablo in the flesh was neither swimming nor floating.

Pablo the spirit saw Ruggy however, bobbing face down in the rising water under the pouring dark sky. The Paradiso sign Ruggy had painted himself floated by in the white caps of the crashing waves. This hurricane had been long overdue. It was time for the earth and the ocean to face each other. It was nature's way of moving something out of itself, releasing the dark part of its soul so the body could survive, clean and at peace.

But it was time for Pablo to return. To go back to Jucélia, and Jorge, and Claudia. He called to them as the electric sensations between worlds began to fade. He was drifting higher and further away from himself. Soon after, light glowed white and warm around his floating body. A flood of whispers from everyone who had ever lived, and all of those yet to be born, in languages never spoken closed in around him. They embraced him, suspending him in a crystalline web, no longer stretched, but cradled. He had no form, and the wash of colors, all bands of yellow and gold and orange and pink bathed his nebulous shape. He rose higher until a thousand fingers belonging to a thousand hands supported his drifting ever upward. The hands decreased to only a few, these belonging to his grandparents and uncles and his father and mother. Though he couldn't see them, he sensed them, feathery like a cloud underneath, yet rooted to them in spirit, as though they were all an unbroken sphere of benevolent light. Their hands lifted him until he was by himself, though not alone. He'd never be alone again.

When he was young and would thumb to the end of *Don Quixote* at Claudia's house, just to find out what happened to the crazy knight, he was sad, not because the knight had died, but because his innocent soul might wander as aimlessly as it had on earth.

But that wouldn't happen here, not in this endless light. There was no worry about what to do here. Worry did not exist at all. Nor did any bad thought, or evil energy. There were no ghosts. Everything you had held onto, good or bad, any fear that had eaten at you, any guilt you wrestled with, and whether they were deep rooted or just in your recent memory, they all vanished. The slate was clean. The nothingness was everything, and the everything was all inside of you.

If it could be explained as a feeling, it was love, but to a degree so high it was unexplainable. That was the mystery. That there was no answer was the solution. There, at last, the soul set free, forever meant nothing.

-The End-

12 - MICHIGAN

MARCOS SHAKES HIS HEAD. HIS EYES are damp, the puffed purple lid of his right side shines with his tears.

"She killed you? I mean, she killed Pablo. Why? Why would she do that?"

"Death is the ultimate victory. It means no more suffering."

"That is true. Look at us, we're almost dead," Marcos says.

"Would that be better?"

"What about our families? What about Joanne?" Marcos says.

All I can do is exhale. "What about you?"

Marcos looks at the papers on my lap. "At least you received something."

"I'm praying for you," I tell him. "I'm praying for us."

Yolanda comes back, just as she said, this time with an ICE agent.

"Time to go back to work," they say.

And so we go.

WITH SOME OF THE SMALL pay I've saved; I buy some lined paper, envelopes, and stamps and write back to Joanne. Her address both inspired and terrified me. It was the town in which I had found life and where my life had ended. 6642 Ivanhoe Avenue, #3, La Jolla, CA.

Joanne's envelope confirmed where I have been. 7488 Calzada de la Fuente, San Diego, CA. As though we are nothing but resources. Supplies.

Hola Joanne,

Recibí tu carta. Gracias por escribirme. Tus palabras me salvaron. Estoy aquí, en el cárcel, no sé dónde estoy exactamente. Pero por favor ayudame. Tengo un amigo aquí que también necesita ayuda. Te extraño. Espero tu respuesta. Te espero.

Osvaldo

More weeks have passed, and I debate sending another note to Joanne. Did she not receive the first one? I had this fantasy that when I was in the infirmary, I would receive more letters from her, but nothing returned. The injuries from Agent Lovato—I haven't seen him around—are aching memories. A ghost in the form of a constant low back throb, my ribs irritable spirits that make me wheeze now and then, make it hard to laugh, not that I have reasons to. The other demon, that tear deep inside my pelvis? Exorcised, at least for now and I worry it will come back one day.

I dreamed the other night I was crawling in a tunnel with Marcos in the lead, escaping the detention center. The tunnel was getting smaller and tighter, dirt falling on my head and into my eyes. The crawlspace was so narrow I couldn't breathe, and then Marcos disappeared. I woke moaning for help, a slight twinge of pain in that spot in my hips. One of the guards, I don't remember which, because I still want to thank him for giving me an ice pack.

Marcos had recovered quickly, but he didn't sign up for many jobs. What's the point of earning anything, he said, if you're not going anywhere? He used to kick the fútbol, join a match often during our one-hour outside breaks, but he began sitting, walking slower around the inside perimeter by himself.

It was all made worse when he was, at last, assigned an attorney. Marcos had leapt up when the young lawyer, a man not much older than Marcos had come for him on visitor day. The attorney was good, could speak Spanish, but by the second visit, he let Marcos know what he feared most. His children were gone. They had been taken to a care center in Michigan.

When Marcos told me, said it was Michigan, a hidden anger boiled inside of me. There it was again, this place I knew nothing about, but had already had a terrible understanding of. It was the place where my first love was once violated, where the villain of her book, the luchador himself—though only a character—was from. Lester Brooks. Ruggy. I imagined awful people there, caging Marcos's children. But he said they were probably with a family—people who were watching his kids as though they were his own. That broke him.

Consoling him with the jokes he said to me didn't work. The boy was pained more than I could know. I stayed with him, walked with him. Reminded him there was hope. One day, Marcos said, "I don't know. Maybe I need to go into that cell for the one's they think will commit suicide."

"Don't make me beat the shit out of you, too," I told him, grabbing his orange jump suit.

"Calm down, tío. I won't."

I gave him what money I had made. It was my turn to feel sorry for myself, nothing from Joanne. At least Marcos had a visitor, an attorney.

And then it came, as unexpected as that note when I was in the infirmary. An ICE agent had come to me on a Friday—the day the visitors are permitted twenty-five-minute time slots—that I, yes, me, Osvaldo Reyes, had one coming. The officer said *she* would be there at 2:45.

13 - VISITOR DAY

I CAN'T REALLY DRESS UP WHEN I'M in an orange suit from head to toe, my feet in browning white socks and flimsy slip-on chanclas for the shower. I hadn't had a haircut—didn't find a reason—but that last wavelet of hair stemming from my cowlick at the back of my head had grown, and it needed a good spit pasting to my bare scalp. Thank God I had shaved with those razors as blunt as they were. It didn't matter at this point what I looked like. She was here. She was coming.

Marcos had said to just go where they tell you to go on Visitor Day. He said it's in a small room with glass windows and a phone with ICE watching and listening to everything on our side, and a big open room on the visitors' side. It's just another border, he said. And time, he said, goes faster there.

A group of seven or eight of us shuffle from the caged areas down a series of corridors, ICE officers flank us, walking slower to make us walk slower. This area doesn't look familiar. They must not want us to remember the way out, or to know that there is indeed another side of the wall.

I wait my turn, my stomach tumbling again from nerves, and from the fruit drink they gave with lunch. It was kind of like a licuado—a smoothie—they called it. I had seen a shop that sold only these near where I used to work at Sea of Cortez. Whatever was in it made my insides grumble. I worry I'll have to ask to go to the bathroom when it's my turn to see Joanne.

She's why I'm so nervous. It's like the night in La Jolla, except now I'm embarrassed instead of excited. She'll be walking in on me, exposed like this. I can't be presentable in this way. I am at my worst here. But at least she's here, por fin.

"Reyes," an officer calls. It's my turn.

No one sits on the other side, and no one moves into view through the glass. Does this count against my time? Waiting for the other person with officers coming into view, there's two in uniform and another person, no uniform. They're talking like they know each other. They walk up toward my window. The one in street clothes is her, Daisy. Desiree Baca.

She doesn't smile, just a quick nod. How is this grown woman the same girl I chatted with through the food hopper at Sea of Cortez? She was so curious and innocent then. We ate lunches together. I told her everything.

She picks up her phone, points to mine on my side. I push my chair out and turn away. I'm not talking to her. To hell with her, but ICE walks me back. Daisy has stood up. She's motioning me to come back. She points to the phone.

Phone to the side of my face, a quiet respiration fills my ear. I grit my teeth and tense my body. I'm going to scream at her, let her have every ounce of hate I have inside me, I'm going to pour my rage on her and let it burn her the way she burned me. But I don't. The sound of her breath and the silence between us cuts deeper than any curse I could send to her through those wires. She stares into me, not saying anything.

"What do you want?" I say.

"Osvaldo," her eyes soften. "I came to say—you're going to get out soon. Your friend, the writer, she kept calling until she found me. And the couple, López, they knew you, and they called me, too. I told them you were here at Otay, that you might be eligible to post bond. The author lady said she was getting an attorney. I sent her to the Department of Homeland Security. You're not seeking asylum. We caught you here, not at the border. You have a better case."

"But why you? Why are you telling me this?"

"Because I know I hurt you."

"Why?"

"This is my—"

"Your job? Why not just tell me, when we ate, or when you asked all those questions? Or when you told me about your life? Why? Why not help me?"

"It's the workplace raids. That's where we're focusing. That and the asylum seekers. Osvaldo, our country can't handle more aliens. You're invasive to our system."

"Chinga la sistema! That's all I hear: the system. Just let me walk out of here and I'll go. I want to leave. I don't want to be here."

"Osvaldo, calm down. Sit down." She switches over to Spanish.

"No, I'm not sitting down. And talk to me in your language. I understand. I'm not stupid."

"You're going to be deported, or you can stay a while longer and plead your case. If you take the help."

"I don't want help. Leave. Go now."

"Osvaldo, look, I love my country. I signed up to do this job. I liked you at first because you were nice. But I was feeling pressured. We were going to bust Sea of Cortez for a while. It was where you and other ones worked. We can't let them go on violating our laws. That's not fair."

"You don't tell me about what's fair. You're out there living your life, and I'm in here in a cage. Get away from me."

"Fine, fair enough. I came today to let you know that I can help, but I won't. I thought you would listen, but you proved to me why this country doesn't like illegal crossers. You act like this is your home."

"Daisy, or whoever you are, nothing is fair. You're young. You think this world can be perfect. No, it can't. Not with liars. Good luck. I wish you a good life."

I hang up the phone, and step back. She stands, her breathing is her only movement. She's a person, she's not evil. I know she's not. She's an innocent human being underneath everything—just like me.

I take the phone. She picks hers back up.

"Forgive me. I'm angry."

"I know. This place is—it is what it is."

"You Americans and how you describe things."

"It was nice to know you, Osvaldo. I do wish you luck."

"I miss the girl from Sea of Cortez."

"I know. Two different people. I can't be both."

"I know. You know who you are. Be that."

"Bye, Osvaldo."

"Bye, Daisy."

We hang up. She stands, stays, and waits for me. I look back, and she's still there. Maybe she wants to be in here. Maybe she should. I turn away, walk ahead, and I hope to never see her again.

VISITOR DAY TURNED INTO another day, and then another, and another. Soon, two more weeks had passed. Some days were good, other days were bad. Rolling off of my cot each morning in itself was work. The work, thankfully kept me busy. Marcos kept me smiling. His lawyer was making progress, and Marcos began to pull out of his depression. No guarantees though, it's the system.

The hour outdoor breaks were the only form of peace. The sky above was the closest I could get to some place like home. Over those walls was the next place. Not Mexico. Not yet. I needed to look up more like this when I was outside. I could imagine myself flying, my spirit floating away like Pablo Garza.

The announcement came early one morning, as I had settled into some kitchen work. One of the nameless, faceless agents—noticeable only by their uniforms, not like Daisy—Desiree Baca—who could blend in. This one was a woman though. She pulled me aside at one of the dishwashing stations. I had eaten that morning, dumped my scraps, and was now washing mine and everyone else's portioned plates and silverware.

"You have a visitor today," she said. "3 PM. We'll come get you."

Marcos, not far from me with a scrubbing pad over the burners on an industrial stove, whistled.

"Tu novia?"

I shrug. No promises. No guarantees. The system. The system.

14 - OTRA VEZ

SITTING AT THE THICK GLASS, IT HITS ME: this is how it's supposed to be.
Together, but apart. Close, but separated. We may never be one body, as the
sacrament of marriage requires. If this is how I must be with her, then so be it.

I open my eyes, close them, then open them again, just to make sure what
I am seeing is real. We don't speak to each other for a while, no phone to
either of our ears, our eyes saying everything. I missed you. I'm sorry. But I
remember this is a waste of the little time we have. I am on the clock. I am
still being watched. She picks up the phone receiver. I pick up mine.

"Osvaldo," she says. "I've been trying to find you for so long. They don't
make this easy."

"Joanne, how long has it been?"

"Almost six months." She opens a folder, shuffles through papers. "You
can get out. I have an attorney who's talking to a judge. I'm trying to get
your bond lowered."

"Thank you" I cry, "Thank you."

"You could show up to court and they could release you then."

"When?"

"They have to set a date. I'm hoping soon."

"Then what?"

"You might enter the United States again and try your case. You can
start over again here. Start the naturalization process. Or they could . . .
remove you. But I don't think that will happen. You're not a criminal. Are
you? Osvaldo, the end is in sight. You're almost free."

She's beautiful. Beautiful for doing this. On the inside and out. And yet, I don't know her. She's a stranger, an alien herself. My only knowledge of her was what I left at the beginning.

"I know this is a lot," she says. "But now I know where you are. I don't want to lose you again."

At the bookstore, I noticed no ring on her finger. But I have to ask. I must know. I want to do this right.

"Joanne, I miss you, and I want to be together. This is, like a dream. Are you, alone? Do you have a . . . husband?"

Joanne hides her eyes, sorts her papers back into the folder.

"There's plenty of time to talk about that. They're waving at me. It's almost time for me to go."

"Don't go. Will you come back? What's next?"

"Don't worry," she says.

"The system."

She nods her head, touches the glass.

"Here, I'm going to give this to you," she says. "They took it away from you that night in La Jolla. ICE said you can have it back, if you want it." She holds up a copy of her new book. The signed copy I had bought at the bookstore.

"Does it have the story you gave me? Slip Soul?"

"Yes, but the one you have is the old ending. This one is new."

MORE DAYS PASS AND Marcos and I are on different schedules again. When I see him at breakfast one day, he says he has news for me and wants to meet on a break in the yard.

"I have something for you, too," I tell him.

In the hot, open and dusty yard, the tall walls topped with razor wire, Marcos gives me a hug. It's a father's hug you only get a few times in your life. It's the embrace of good luck, goodbye, I love you, I'll miss you. The hug of knowing that you don't belong to each other—you never have—but that you will always help your fellow man. It's the soldier hug, the warrior embrace, the letting go of the pain you have both endured. Although he's younger than me that doesn't seem to matter. He's the one that's been caring for me in here, listening to my every word, helping me remember that I'm still worth something. He's been the father figure all along. He has a light inside of him that never goes out.

"I have a court date next week," he says. "The attorney says it will go fast. My wife made it over. She's with our children."

"In Michigan?"

"Yes."

"What's your plan? Are you going to live there?"

"No, fuck this country. We're going to Canada, tío," he says.

"Pinche Marcos, you make me laugh until the end." I look at him, "Take a jacket. It snows there."

"I don't care if the sky pisses on me, I just want to be with my family. But tío, serious, I want you to get out, too. Now that your novia found you, she can get you out, no?"

"We'll see."

"What's that you have?"

"Her book, the real one. You still want to hear how it ends?"

"Yes, read it to me."

I flip to the end, the last chapter.

Slip Soul by Joanne McCasey Watson
Chapter 16

The storm passed in the early morning hours and took with it all of the clouds and rain that had built up for the last day and a half. The ocean had swallowed up the remains of Paradiso and sent Lester Brooks' body far and deep into the Pacific. The beach and streets were empty, recovering in silence from the violent storm, the real paradise shaken and bruised, but not dead.

The sun shone bright into the picture window at Los Bungalows de las Brisas. Jucélia, Renata, Claudia, and Jorge had stayed there through the night as the storm raged on. Pablo had not returned. The Bungalows suffered little damage because Pablo had set sandbags out the night before. They laughed wondering when he had a chance to do it. Maybe, they said, when he was asleep, all of them now aware of his gift.

But Jucélia remained inconsolable. Claudia tended to her with teas and cold cloths on her forehead. Renata had cleaned up the patio that was filled with leaves from the palapa, and Jorge checked out guests and swept the water back to the *malecón*. Pablo didn't return that day, or the next. Jucélia's tears continued, but Claudia wouldn't let her mourn—she said it wasn't time.

In the days after the storm, peace and calm had returned—the beach and town looked like nothing had ever happened. As though there had never been a man named Lester "Ruggy" Brooks, or his bar Paradiso, or that a certain soul called Pablo Garza, the good man with a power to leave his skin, had ever existed.

Not so at Los Bungalows de las Brisas. Claudia made sure to keep Pablo alive with music playing in the palapa, guests still checking in, and she brought Jucélia along with her to keep the young lady from staying in bed.

"What is something that gives you joy?" Claudia had asked Jucélia in those days.

"My journal. I like to write," Jucélia said.

"Then write," Claudia said. "Imagine your future. Imagine your life in five years, ten years. Write that down. Write to your lover. Write to you unborn child."

This made Jucélia cry even more, but Claudia had her ways, and so she sent Jucélia to sit and write.

Jucélia stopped Claudia to ask her, "Did you want children?"

Claudia lowered her eyelids, tilted her head. "I have them already. You. Renata. Jorge. Pablo. You're all my children."

Claudia hugged her close and they shared a long cry. Claudia got Jucélia some water and a pen from the front desk.

"Remember, say anything you want," Claudia walked Jucélia back to Pablo's apartment, then tucked her in with a blanket to let her rest.

"Will you stay?" Jucélia said, "Here in town with us."

"Oh, *mi amor*," Claudia said, "my home is in the mountains. You are welcome there anytime. For as long as you want."

"Not yet," Jucélia said. "Not yet."

"Whenever you're ready." Claudia turned and left Jucélia. She opened the journal and began to write.

If I ever have a son, I will name him Paolo. If I have a daughter, I will name her Rosinha, after my mother. Or maybe Paola. Maybe Paola Rosinha or Rosinha Paola. Both sound nice. I've always liked that name. I wonder what it will be like to carry a baby in my belly. How it will feel to have a little life growing inside of me. I will sing and talk to it, and dance with it.

I will tell you about your mother, baby. I am Jucélia Maria Duran, 24-years-old from São Paolo, Brazil. My skin is black, and my hair is long and curly. I'm not very tall, and I'm thin. I came here to Mexico, to Puerto Escondido to start a new life. I came with your aunt Renata, my sister. This was supposed to be a stop on the way to the United States. That was where I wanted to go, to one day to become a teacher. But this place—Oaxaca— was so beautiful and magical—that we stayed. I hope we can stay here forever. I would like for you to grow up here. You will be half Afro-Brazilian and half Mexican. This will be your home, and you will always have a home in Brazil. You are home, here inside of me.

About your father. His name is Pablo Domingo Garza. He was born and raised here in Puerto Escondido and grew up here at the beach, Playa Zicatela. He is the son of Domingo and Eva Garza, who built and operated this very motel where I am sitting now. It's a little white adobe inn with twenty rooms and it's very close to the beach. From here you can see the ocean. You can almost reach out and touch it. It's called Los Bungalows de Las Brisas.

Jucélia stopped to wipe the tears streaming down her face and to blot those that had fallen on to the paper. Claudia wanted her to keep writing to distract her from what they all feared. If this was her fate, she knew she would have to face it, and eventually move on. Look at Claudia, such strength and energy after everything she had endured in her life. That's what all of this was about, endurance. That's what life was, anyway. How long you could take it.

Noises came from the other side of the bedroom door, commotion of some kind. Jucélia figured it was Jorge and a new guest, check-in tended to be a noisy affair with boards dropping to the floor, bags set down, people in awe of the simple rustic beauty of the motel. Jucélia sat up to go see, then decided to sit back again. There was a slight tap on the bedroom door.

"Come in," she said.

The doorknob turned, and the door pushed open slowly. Like a washed-up merman from the sea, hair damp and tangled with foam and kelp, skin blackened with sand, Pablo, stepped into the room. His eyes deep pools of brown, stunned but alive, so alive, he ran to Jucélia and embraced her, whispering into her ear, tears streaming down their faces.

-The End-

15 - HOMELAND

"SHE SAVED HIM," MARCOS SAYS. "He came back."

"He came back."

"See, there are happy endings," Marcos says.

"Yours is starting now, mi sobrino."

"Don't worry about me," he says. "Just get out of here already and go see your vieja girlfriend. Make love to her tonight. It still works, no?"

I hit his shoulder, then mess with his hair. His life is beginning again.

"Be safe," I say. "That's all that matters."

We lift our chins to each other, acknowledge this moment, this place in time when we will never see each other again, where the only path forward for the other person is a distant, blurry vision of their own future—the closest thing to a real, touchable version of faith.

AND SO, MY MOMENT arrives, too. Weeks after Marcos had left, another visitor day turns into the release. The agents and Joanne, help me, usher me away to the outside. Leaving this place, I wish that all the souls trapped inside may find their own release, that they may travel far away over the beaches and oceans unchained, their spirits free, crossing back to where they want to be, souls and bodies united.

JOANNE'S HOME IN LA JOLLA is small. A townhouse she calls it. Two bedrooms, a narrow kitchen, and a small balcony that looks up a hillside covered in mansions. I have nothing to unpack, nothing to put away. She shows me to a bedroom with a bathroom.

"First, I need to make a call home," I say.

She hands me her phone. "Take your time," she says.

I call Felipe and I sob into the phone and tell him everything. He understands. I tell him I will see him soon.

Now washed and dressed—Joanne had bought me a fresh set of clothes—I emerge. Joanne takes my hand, hugs me. I'm electrified, almost shivering. She places her hand on my heart, touches her forehead to mine.

This is starting from the very beginning. Even before we first met on the zócalo. This is a blind date. This is not a customer, a client, a student, it's not Teresa. It's not Jucélia or Renata or Tía Claudia. This is a saint, my patroness. Though, she won't let me say anything like that. On the ride back into San Diego, she brushed off everything I said about paying her back for the bond. That it wasn't much anyway. It will all wash out, she kept saying.

"We're going for a walk. You need air, sunshine. I'm going to take you where I was going to take you after my reading."

In the café, people peck away on their computers, others reading, some talk, laugh, listen with care, as though they have been doing all these things for months, without interruption, going about their lives while I went about mine.

A young waiter brings the drinks while Joanne and I sit in silence, facing each other, studying one another. We break each other's stares and look away, or down into our cups. Where do we start?

"How long has it been?" she says. "Since before they took you? How many years?"

I shrug. "Treinta y cinco? Forty?"

"It's just amazing," Joanne says. "To be sitting here, looking at you."

"I like the book. New ending, it's beautiful and sad."

"Thank you." She blushes. "I can't believe you kept the original one."

"It's my—¿cómo se dice?—tesoro?"

"Your treasure, you are so sweet. Thank you."

Her left hand hugs her cup. No ring on her finger.

"So, you married?"

"Was. I was married. My husband passed away."

"I'm sorry."

"It was a while ago," she says.

"My wife passed away last year."

"Oh," She covers her mouth, then rests her hand on mine.

"Cancer. How did your husband go?"

Joanne pulls her hand off her cup. She clasps her hands and places them in her lap. She looks straight at me, and I know I shouldn't have asked this question.

"He committed suicide."

I close my eyes and hold my stomach to keep it from sinking.

"It's okay. Really, it's okay," she says. "He had depression and other problems."

"I'm sorry I asked."

"No, it's better to talk about it anyway. He was just—we ended up not being a good match. But we did have our good times. It wasn't all bad. It changed as time went on. When I started publishing, he grew jealous. Started threatening me, said he'd leave me because I was busy traveling and promoting my work. The problem was I didn't realize he'd been like that our whole marriage, keeping tabs on me, and saying I spent too much time writing and not with him. But you know, he was just as busy. He wanted to be the Mayor. He got on the City Council and that was a miserable failure. He made enemies, got some bad press. Got involved with the religious type. That's what got to him—and seeing me succeed. I supported everything he did, but I guess that's not what he wanted. He drank, too, but kept that a secret. That didn't help. I guess he was like my character, you know, Ruggy. He didn't assault me, but the words hurt. Almost just as bad and you can never take them back."

Pobrecita Joanne. Not the girl I met so long ago. She was now a grown woman with years of hardship. And yet, she's so peaceful. So at ease.

"It's hard, like you say. When my wife died, our family broke. It takes a long time to feel better."

"It takes years. Sometimes it never heals." She breathes in, her chest rising and falling so calm, the movement comforts me.

"So how did you find me? And how long had you been in San Diego?" she says.

"I had a work visa, a J-7. I worked at the Faith Mission Center in artesania."

"The center that closed. I know it well," she says. "Steve, my late husband, was part of that. He was an investor. It all seemed like a bad idea."

"I have to tell you, I found that place looking for you. I thought maybe . . ."

"Oh, Osvaldo. We just lost touch, and people our age don't do well with keeping names and addresses. I thought about you often. You always came to me in my dreams."

"This feels like one," I say.

"And after the Faith Mission Center, how—"

"I knew someone who said I might find work at Sea of Cortez. I went there for a few weeks before my visa ran out. There I met Daisy. Well, her name is Desiree."

"The ICE agent? Oh, Osvaldo, I'm so sorry. It's bad here. There's no sympathy for immigrants."

"I know. That's why I want to leave."

"But you can't now. Not yet, you're on bond. You have a court date."

"I'll think about it."

"I, I just want you to be safe."

"I'm safe now. You're why I'm here."

A gasp, just loud enough for me to hear it, escapes her lips. She sits back some. I've scared her.

"I don't know what to say," Joanne says.

"Nothing, that was all I want to say to you. I always wanted to find you again, and here you are."

I wait. I've always waited. I've always let her show the way. Back in Oaxaca City and Puerto Escondido and Baja, I let her reveal herself, as much or as little as she wanted. And I never rushed her. I only waited.

"When I met you in Oaxaca City that first time," she says, "I knew you were someone special. I knew what you did, I had heard of zócalo boys, I wasn't stupid, but I wasn't looking for anything—no sex—just a friend. And I found that. I found that with you."

"Did you think what I did was dirty? Is that why you stopped writing letters?"

"Not at all; I guess, I thought I would never see you again. I just, moved on."

"I remember your last letter. You were a teacher. You had someone in your life."

Joanne searches, her eyelids fluttering.

"Maybe, I . . . I don't remember. There was only one man before I met my husband."

"You know, that time in Baja California—I thought, maybe we . . . make a b—"

Her face tightens up, she reaches for the napkin by her tea. She grips the thin paper, brings it to her delicate skin, and wipes a tear. I've forgotten everything I knew about how to treat a woman.

"Juana, I'm sorry, I'm so sorry. I don't mean to—"

"No, no, it's me. I'm sorry. I never had children. I mean, I could have, but—we just never did. And no, that time, you and me. I didn't get pregnant. That was my first time after I was . . . I'm sorry, it still hurts me. What about you? Tell me about you? Do you have children?"

"Yes, one son. That's who I called at your home. He didn't know where I've been all this time. My wife and I tried for more, but God only gave us one. My son also has one son."

"That's truly a blessing, you're a lucky man. You always have been."

"I'm lucky you helped me. And I'm lucky you are still my friend."

"I will always be your friend."

The noise of the café quiets around me. I see her and only her, almost glowing, and I know now that she was the one in those dreams I sometimes have where I felt the presence of another. But that's all they are, dreams.

"I have to go."

"Now?" she says. "Where?"

"I want to return to Mexico, my own way."

"But immigration and homeland security . . . They—"

"No, they won't miss me. One less person to worry about."

"But how?"

"I remember the way. From here to Baja, Baja to Mexico, Mexico to Oaxaca."

I stand, my body not aching, and I breathe in the air of this enchanted place, knowing it's not real, that it's just been a place to stay, and that now, at last, it's time to check out—to go through the hidden door one last time. But I don't want to leave her just sitting here alone. I want this moment to continue. I want this newness to go on and on, but not here.

"You know the way, too." I take her hand and bring her to her feet. "Will you join me?"

We're not the same people we once were. Our faces, our bodies, and hair have aged. Our skin is stained with dark spots, and the bones in our bodies have also weakened with age. But our souls are young and free to roam. They're not held to anything. They can soar now into the sky, orbs of pure light bouncing, then bending into unbreakable beams intertwined, nothing holding them down, and nothing encasing their infinite energy.

She stands, holds my hand with a grip I've never felt. A grip that says she's never letting go. She nods and whispers, "I will."

-EL FIN-

ACKNOWLEDGEMENTS

My sincerest thanks to those who have read this story throughout its development and who have inspired me to keep going: Dorothy Waite, Rodolfo Rivera, Susan Lawson, Jeremy Lawson, and Kathryn Wilson. Thank you to Sheri Williams and Ashley Carlson for having faith in my work, and to Analieze Cervantes for your insights, guidance, and kind support through every step. To my large and colorful family, thank you all. And for mis corazones, Bonnie and my boys: thank you always for your love, encouragement, and for supporting this thing I do.

And to all the traveling souls at the border, whether you are young, old, coming, or going, here to stay or passing through, you are human and deserve to be treated with dignity, mercy, and love. May your travels be safe, may you find what you seek, and may you always be protected and loved.

ABOUT THE AUTHOR

TAYLOR GARCIA is the author of the short story collection *Functional Families,* and other stories and essays. Taylor García's short stories and essays have appeared in *Chagrin River Review, Driftwood Press, Fifth Wednesday Journal, Hawaii Pacific Review, McSweeney's Internet Tendency, Caveat Lector, Writing Disorder, Diverse Voices Quarterly, 3AM Magazine, Evening Street Review* and others. He also writes the weekly column, "Father Time," at the Good Men Project, and holds an MFA from Pacific University Oregon. García is a multi-generational *Neomexicano* originally from Santa Fé, New Mexico now living Southern California with his wife and children.

Connect with the author at www.btaylorgarcia.com
Twitter @btaylorgarcia

Made in the USA
Las Vegas, NV
17 November 2021

34668234R00116